Elena's Memory

Rachele Modiano Mendes Investigates
Book 1

Silvano Stagni

Perpetuum Mobile Limited

Copyright © 2023 by Silvano Stagni

ISBN 978-1-7393596-6-9

This novel is entirely a work of fiction. The names, characters and incidents portrayed in it are the work of the author's imagination. Any resemblance to actual persons, living or dead, events or localities is entirely coincidental.

Cover by Coverjig

By the same author

The Dressmaker's Parcels

The story of the Modiano Mendes clan during Mussolini's racial laws, World War II, and the Holocaust. Spoiler: Rachele and her eldest daughter Emma join the resistance.

Available on Amazon

Unconditional

A collection of feel good short stories about acceptance, love, and memories.

Available on Amazon

Reflections in the Water

1921. Rachele Modiano starts working for a Venetian law firm after she married Gabriele Mendes. Her first case turns into a web of fraud, blackmail, and possibly murder. Rachele must win over a magistrate who dismisses her as an aristocrat toying with the law as a hobby and protect her client's name. First book in the series "Rachele Modiano, the early years."

Available on Amazon

✺ Created with Vellum

*To all those who had to walk through an emotional thunderstorm
and made it to see sunshine and blue sky.*

Foreword

The Mendes clan

Samuele Mendes (born 1870), **Fiamma Andrade** (born 1873)

- **Raffaele Mendes** (born 1895), married to **Antonella Levi** - their children: **Carlo Mendes** (b. 1923), **Fiamma Mendes** (b. 1926), **Andrea Mendes** (b. 1928)
- **Gabriele Mendes** (born 1897), married to **Rachele Modiano** - their children: **Emma Mendes** (b. 1924), **Anna Mendes** (b. 1926). **Diana Mendes** (b.1929), **Leo Mendes** (b.1932), **Davide Mendes** (b. 1934), **Mila Mendes** (b. 1943)
- **Emanuele Mendes** (born 1902), married to **Gemma Mustaki** - their children: **Mario Mendes** (b. 1932), **Paola Mendes** (b. 1934)
- **Myriam Mendes** (born 1905), married to **Michele Bolaffi** - their children: **Enrico Bolaffi** (b. 1930), **Gloria Bolaffi** (b.1936)
- **Roberto Mendes** (born 1913), married to **Dina Pirani** - their child: **Silvio Mendes** (Born 1948).

Samuele Mendes was arrested in 1943. He died on the train taking him to Auschwitz. Raffaele Mendes and his family moved to Canada in 1939, and Emanuele Mendes and his wife were shot while trying to escape after being arrested in 1943. Their children, Mario and Paola, survived and live with Gabriele and Rachele. Michele Bolaffi (Myriam's husband) survived the camps but struggles with the memories. Emma Mendes married Roberto Sonnino in 1946 after he started working for an oil company. During the time covered in this story, they live in Venezuela.

More information about what happened to the Mendes clan during World War II can be found in my other book "The Dressmaker's Parcels"

Chapter One

November 1947

Deborah Camerini, Countess Pesaro de Bonfili, was walking back from La Fenice opera house with her childhood friend Fiamma Andrade Mendes, her friend's son Roberto Mendes, and his wife Dina.

They had enjoyed the performance, and they were still discussing it. Deborah was pleased to see Fiamma so lively, a rare occurrence since the end of the war. They arrived near her home and it was time to part company. Roberto looked at his wife.

"Did you tell Aunt Deborah?"

"I thought you did. You didn't? Why?"

The countess thought they were joking, but it was also late.

"Tell me what?"

Dina looked at her husband.

"Men!"

"Men, what? I thought you wanted to tell people."

The countess lack of patience was common knowledge among her family and close friends. Roberto was her honorary nephew, her handsome golden boy. But even golden boys do not necessarily take a hint. Fiamma was looking at the scene and could see her honorary sister getting impatient, and she thought she had kept their secret long enough.

"OK. I'll tell her. Dina is pregnant. The baby is due in the spring."

The countess hugged them, then turned to her honorary sister.

"How long have you known? Why did you keep it from me?"

She then turned to Dina

"I am so happy for you. I remember how happy I was when I realised I was pregnant with Giorgio after almost two years of marriage."

She wished them all good night. Hugged everybody again, opened the door into the internal courtyard of the building and waved at them before closing the door. As she was climbing the two flights of steps to her home, her mind turned to the letter she had received from the Red Cross that morning.

"We tried again, but we have no information on the whereabouts or the death of Raffaele Mustaki, Sylvia Schwartz, or their daughter, Leah Mustaki."

It sounded final. The countess walked into her home, took off her coat, and entered the study, poured herself a drink to warm up, sat at the desk, and opened the bottom drawer to her right. She picked up two folders. One had 'Last will of Raffaele Mustaki' on its cover, and the other 'Last will of Sylvia Schwartz Mustaki'. She carefully placed them on the desk, her right hand caressing the name on the cover of each folder. It was time to call the cavalry, her honorary nephew Roberto and Rachele, the wife of his brother Gabriele, another honorary nephew.

On her way to her bedroom, she thought of her cunning matchmaking plans for her son, Giorgio. Rachele Modiano, one of the youngest children of a Jewish aristocratic family from Trieste, would make the perfect wife for the future Count Pesaro de Bonfili. Her mistake was to invite Gabriele as well; he and Rachele looked at each other, and the world around them stopped existing. Her cunning plan had not worked. Later, she realised they would have clashed. They had grown fond of each other at a distance. That would not have happened in a mother-in-law/daughter-in-law relationship. She liked and loved Rachele as her honorary niece.

A formidable woman in her early seventies, the countess still looked impeccable at every moment of the day, still wore high heels and could murder somebody with a polite phrase. She thought of her 'legal cavalry' as she changed into a nightdress and matching nightgown and sat at the dresser to remove her make-up and prepare her face for the night. By the time she was ready for bed, she was sure they would sort things out and find the legal heirs; it was time to pay them a visit.

The same day, in a displaced people camp in Northern Germany, Rav Lazar and his wife were waiting for a young woman to arrive for dinner. Leah Mustaki's personal hell did not end when the Allied troops liberated the camp. Months in a US Army hospital brought her back to acceptable levels of weight, stamina, and health. Ruth Lazar was aware that she and her husband represented the closest thing to a family Leah had. They often talked about her, that evening was not an exception. They were discussing her as Ruth was laying the table.

"Do you have any idea why Leah is in no hurry to leave the camp?"

Rav Lazar lifted his head from the book he was reading

"She has lost her memory. Leah lives in the present and changes the subject whenever somebody tries to talk about her past."

Ruth Lazar looked at the table, then at her husband

"What do doctors say?"

Rav Lazar looked for something he could use as a bookmark before closing the book.

"It is difficult to establish a physical cause for her memory loss. There is a discrepancy between her name and the name the Nazi registered in their ledger next to the number they tattooed on her forearm. Our doctor are not sure whether they can trust the Nazi records."

"Couldn't be a mistake?"

"Possibly, but unlikely. In the ledger, Leah Mustaki is registered in the following line."

Rav Lazar stood up from his arm-chair to get the kiddush cup, the cup he would use later for the blessing before the meal.

"I hope I can bring up the new British doctor in the camp. Our doctors told me he studied with Freud before the war. He might have some ideas to help her recover her memory."

The table was ready. They were just waiting for Leah and the other guests. Ruth removed her apron. Before she went back to the kitchen to put it away, she turned to her husband.

"I wonder whether Leah is escaping from the memories associated with her real identity."

"You might have a point. "

There was a knock at the door. The first guests had arrived. Rav Lazar went to open the door.

After dinner, Leah stayed to help with clearing up, a great opportunity for Ruth Lazar to talk to her.

"Your doctor told us that the new British doctor could help you. I think it is worth talking to him."

Leah was interested

"I will. I want to overcome the sense of emptiness when I think of what might have happened before I woke up in a hospital bed."

Ruth Lazar saw an opening and continued.

"If the new doctor makes you recover your memory, you may start thinking of a life away from here."

Leah put down a serving platter she had just dried.

"Maybe. I feel useful here because I can speak Italian, French, German, English and Greek, and even some Polish."

She picked up another plate to dry, was silent for a few minutes, then continued.

"It is time to try everything I can to get reacquainted with my past. I know there are doubts that I am Leah Mustaki. Do you know my other identity?"

Ruth did not expect that. She put a glass on the drying rack, dried her hands, and turned towards Leah.

"I think my husband does, but the doctor suggested we do not mention it to you until you recover your memory."

Ruth looked at Leah's face, she realised the young woman was close to tears. She hugged her. Leah hugged her back and hid her head on the rabbi's wife shoulders.

"It is time to do everything I can to get my memory back."

In Vienna, Joshua Schwartz was considering his future. He had joined the US Army in 1942, raised to officer rank, and was in charge of vetting Austrians as part of the de-Nazification process. He liked the city and his investigative job. From time to time, he was also involved in the search for war criminals. Colonel McLaren's secretary came with two folders. He couldn't help but notice Joshua was chasing his thoughts.

"News from home?"

Joshua put the two letters aside and took the folders. He started looking for another folder to send back to the Colonel.

"One is from personnel. They informed me the time has come to decide whether to go home or extend my stay in the Army. The other is from my fiancée."

He found the folder and gave it to the secretary, then added,

"Please tell the Colonel I'll be back in fifteen minutes. I need to take a walk in the park to clear my head. I won't be long."

The weather was not his friend; it was a cold, damp November day. A walk in the park did not seem such a great idea. He walked past a nearby café; on impulse, he went in for a hot chocolate, a luxury in 1947 Vienna. The café was warm and inviting, and the chocolate was welcome. On his way out, he noticed the office cleaner sitting at a table with somebody. He said hello as he walked past, just to be polite, ignoring the cleaner's companion. They noticed him. He returned to his office, sat down, and picked up his fiancée's letter again; he missed her. Joshua reread the letter; it was time to return home and build a life.

Chapter Two

November 1947

The Cantoni-Mendes-Modiano law firm had moved to their new office in Riva De Biasio the previous day. The location was great, opposite the waterbus stop. Venetian clients and clients from the mainland could reach them using the waterbus, or *vaporetto,* as Venetians called it. They were one stop from Venice railway station and two from Piazzale Roma, where cars and buses from the mainland had to stop. Two years after starting a law firm from a room in a café and Rachele's study, they were having coffee in their new offices. The three partners were taking a break from the boxes. They had given precedence to the meeting room facing the Grand Canal and to the entrance hall where the receptionist would sit. Once they had taken care of the "front of the house" for their clients, the rest could wait. Roberto Mendes was standing by the window, explaining his plan to sort out the office. Suddenly, he stopped talking.

"Aunt Deborah just got out of the vaporetto and is about to ring the doorbell."

They and their office did not meet Deborah Camerini's strict standards; they had to act quickly. Rachele stood up, ran out of the room. Alvise started tidying up the meeting room. He turned to Roberto.

"Where has Rachele gone?"

Roberto was folding the office floor plan.

"I think she's gone to her office to pick up her courtroom dress..."

They heard the bathroom door slam shut.

"...and now she is in the bathroom to change."

Roberto picked up the floor plan, his and Rachele's notebooks, and took them to his office on the way to the door. Alvise looked out of the window. They had sprung into action faster than the time it took Countess Deborah Pesaro de Bonfili to cross the Riva, not one of the widest in Venice.

They were ready by the time she had climbed the two flights of steps leading to the office. Calm restored, there was no outward sign of the previous moments of panic. Roberto opened the door.

"Good afternoon, Aunt Deborah. It is so nice to see you."

Roberto kissed her hand. Age had not mellowed Deborah Camerini, Countess Pesaro de Bonfili. It had enhanced her personality traits, both the good ones and the ones her honorary nephew and Rachele found annoying. She walked into the office carrying a briefcase.

Rachele had come out of the bathroom wearing a Chanel two-piece suit and a silk shirt (her court uniform), and Alvise Cantoni, the other partner in the law firm, had checked that the meeting room was neat and tidy. Alvise came out of the meeting room.

"Countess Pesaro De Bonfili, good afternoon."

He shook her hand. Her white hair styled in a 1920s bob barely moved when she gave a disappointed stare at Alvise Cantoni., but shook his hand. Alvise recovered.

"Let me take your coat and your briefcase. I'll put the coat away and take the briefcase to the meeting room."

Deborah Camerini's disapproving look turned into half a smile.

Rachele came out of the bathroom.

"Good afternoon, Aunt Deborah, what a pleasant surprise."

She scanned her honorary niece from head to toe. Rachele had a 26-year-old policy of letting the men of the family deal with her first. The countess loved her honorary nephews and could never disapprove of, or deny anything to, her golden boy, the very handsome Roberto Mendes. She smiled, happy to be ignored but aware that her turn would come.

"Good afternoon to you Rachele. Did Roberto tell you about our night at the Opera? It was so nice to see Fiamma smile. It doesn't happen very often these days."

The countess told Rachele all about the evening. She stopped before they entered the meeting room.

"Isn't it great Dina is expecting? She seems to follow the family pattern, first pregnancy about two years after the wedding."

Rachele took it as the countess meant it. Several women in the Mendes clan had their first child about two years after they got married.

The meeting room had a table, a sofa and two armchairs. Alvise and Rachele took a seat on the armchairs. The countess sat on the sofa and patted the seat beside her, telling Roberto to sit by her side.

"I love the view. You can see the church of Santa Lucia across the Grand Canal. I assume I could also see the entrance into Canal Cannareggio if I stood up."

Then she looked at Rachele, who braced herself, knowing her time had come.

"A Chanel is always a classic, but I would not wear it if I planned to sit on those armchairs; it clashes with the upholstery. You are a very elegant woman. If you must come into this room dressed like that, I suggest sitting on a chair. I would wear dressier shoes, but I understand you are here to unpack boxes, and one must be practical, must one not?"

The countess knew how to sugar-coat criticism with praise. Deborah Camerini asked Alvise to fetch her briefcase. She pulled out two thick folders; they were the reason for her visit.

"Do you remember Raffaele Mustaki? The brother of poor Gemma, Emanuele's wife. Such a shame they were shot, but a blessing if you think they were spared the camps."

There was a pause in the conversation. Rachele and Roberto looked at each other. The painful memory of the faces of Emanuele Mendes and Gemma Schwartz Mendes flashed in their minds. It still hurt to think of the events surrounding the round-up of Venetian Jews. Alvise remarked they had all been lucky to have escaped. The moment of sadness did not stop the countess.

"As you know, Raffaele and Gemma's father was a very close friend of my late husband. Before they left Venice, Raffaele and his wife, Silvia Schwartz, came to give me their wills for safekeeping. I have their wills here; both named me as their executor."

Alvise was the will specialist in the firm.

"What steps did you take to establish what happened to them?"

"I have made enquiries with the Red Cross several times, with no results. They are nowhere to be found. Almost two and a half years after the war, it's time to do something about them. Once everything is sorted out in your office, look at their wills and tell me what I must do."

She dropped the folders on the coffee table and started talking to Roberto. Rachele and Alvise looked at each other; the countess had dismissed them. Rachele got up.

"We shall call you to arrange an appointment as soon as possible once we have read both wills with the attention they deserve."

Alvise sat at the far end of the table in the meeting room, took out the first document, and started to read. Rachele left the room. Rachele did not pay any attention to Roberto's silent plea for help. She left the golden boy to deal with their honorary aunt. Payback may come later, but, for the moment, she was too busy thinking of how she could be very busy somewhere else for the next hour.

After spending an hour with her golden boy, the countess was ready to go. Alvise notice she had stood up and rushed to get her briefcase and help her with her coat.

"We'll call you in a few days to arrange an appointment for next week."

Once they reached the door, Alvise remembered to kiss her hand rather than shake it. Roberto kissed her honorary aunt on the cheek. Rachele came out of her office wearing the trousers and jumper she wore before the countess arrived; she should have known better. Deborah scanned her from head to toe; the final parting comment was hers, as usual.

"Rachele, it is always a pleasure to see you. You are elegant even when being very practical; I love those trousers! Please kiss the children for me."

Later, Gabriele Mendes, Rachele's husband and Roberto's brother joined them after spending his day doing bookkeeping and managing the law firm's finances in their old premises, the ground floor of his mother's house. Roberto stopped taking things out of a box when he heard his brother's voice and joined his brother and his sister-in-law in the hall.

"Did you know aunt Deborah was coming? These two left me alone with her for an hour!"

"I didn't. Organise payback later. You are a handsome young man, and everybody knows aunt Deborah loves the company of attractive young men!"

Gabriele and Rachele had kept up with their habit of taking a walk twice a day since their first child was born. It was their private time; their family was too large to hope for any time for themselves at home. The countess's visit to the firm led them to talk about their nephew and niece.

Mario and Paola Mendes were the children of Gabriele and Roberto's brother Emanuele and his wife, Gemma, the sister of Raffaele Mustaki.

"A letter from the family court arrived this morning. We are now their legal guardians. We also receive another letter with the date for the court hearing to recover their parents' assets that were seized in 1943."

Rachele was silent for a few minutes.

"We do not have to tell them now. Paola still cannot talk about her parents. I would like to talk to Doctor Corinaldi before we discuss it with them."

Gabriele had always been protective of his family, which now included his nephew and niece.

"I agree, but we also do not discuss the Mustaki-Schwarz wills at home. At least not until we know more."

Three days later, the whole firm sat in the meeting room facing the Grand Canal to discuss their strategy with the countess. They placed the countess at the head of the table between two young men, Alex Modiano (Rachele's nephew and one of the firm's researchers) and Franco Cantoni (Alvise's son and the other firm's researcher). A seating strategy that ensured she stayed in a good mood. Her golden boy, Roberto Mendes, was leading the meeting. He was sitting at the other end of the table between the other two partners, his sister-in-law, Rachele, and Alvise Cantoni. The countess was the honorary aunt of the other two people present at the meeting: Gabriele Mendes was the bookkeeper/operation director of the law firm, and Diana Mendes, one of Gabriele and Rachele's six children, was there to take notes. The countess was taking notes as well. After two hours, she stood up with a very sombre face.

"Thank you all; the evening before I brought you the two wills, I thought of you as my legal cavalry. I now know I was right. I am sure that the two hussars sitting on each side of me will find out what happened to Raffaele, Sylvia, and Leah, that Alvise will guide them in their search for the legal heirs, and that Rachele and Roberto will recover all their assets seized by the Fascist state in 1944."

She looked at her notepad before collecting her things.

"Four days ago, I was very pessimistic; now, I am optimistic again. I was right; it was time. Now, Diana, can we compare notes to ensure I wrote everything we have decided?"

Gabriele and Rachele had invited the countess to dinner; she told them she had a few errands to run and would join them later. On their way home, Rachele shared with Gabriele the next step in the charm offensive, asking her advice about what to wear in a meeting in Rome organised by Mario Sonnino, the father-in-law of their eldest daughter, Emma. Rachele would be one of two women out of thirty lawyers and politicians.

"Aunt Deborah is a very elegant woman, used to being a high-profile person. I need her advice. She may be an amateur art dealer, but she is a force to be reckoned with at auctions, even though often she is the only woman."

Gabriele did not agree his wife needed the advice of their honorary aunt.

"Why do you need her advice? You are poised and elegant, come from a very high-profile family and are used to being one of the few women, often the only woman, in a male environment."

Rachele realised that after twenty-six years of marriage, she was still a perfect person in her husband's eyes. She was also very pragmatic.

"I may not need it, but asking her for advice would flatter her, and we have just started a long process. Also, I trust her advice on how a woman should look when she wants to establish that she is not some adornment in the arms of her male companion. I understand she achieves that without looking like somebody trying to impersonate a man."

~

Her calling card was very formal: Deborah Camerini, Countess Pesaro de Bonfili. However, she was 'Aunt Deborah' for Fiamma's children and grandchildren. She was fond of them and always arrived with something for the children. When Anita, the housekeeper, opened the door, she saw this very elegant lady carrying four bags and her handbag.

"Countess Pesaro De Bonfili, welcome. Why didn't you hire a porter?"

Anita was in the inner core of the countess good book for everything she had done to protect the Mendes family and support Fiamma during the racial laws and World War II.

"Good evening, Anita. In the beginning, I did not expect to buy anything big. I wanted to buy a birthday present for Diana, then I thought of all the others and I got carried away."

Once all the parcels were on the floor, she hugged Anita.

"I told you many times to call me Deborah, like everybody else does. Where are the children?"

Anita knew she had better stay formal.

"They are in the large sitting room, Countess Deborah,"

Anita picked up the largest parcels and led the way. As an honorary member of the Mendes clan, Deborah knew that the family's children came first, hence the four bags. She gave Diana a present for her birthday; Anna had not come home yet, Leo and Mario were next, then Davide and Paola and then the countess spent time with Mila.

Rachele stood for some time at the door of the large sitting room watching this very elegant and formidable lady take her high-heeled shoes off, sit on the floor and play with a four-year-old whilst paying attention to what the other children were telling her. After about ten minutes, the countess stood up.

"Now you all have seen how small I am. I have to talk to your mother before dinner."

She put her shoes back on, hugged everyone again and followed her honorary niece. Once they were in the bedroom with the wardrobe doors wide open, Rachele explained why she needed help.

"In Rome, I will be one of two women at the conference and at the dinner in the evening. The other one is a politician. I want to convey that I am not a 'female lawyer'; I am a lawyer who happens to be a woman."

The countess knew what she meant.

"Start with the shoes, and wear the highest heels you own. You can wear dark colours but add bright coloured accessories. It shows boldness and confidence. Show me your highest-heeled shoes; then we will look at a dress for the dinner and a suit for the conference."

Rachele started taking shoes out; she was never one for high heels. Her collection of shoes did not impress the countess.

"I know that your mother can look down on somebody twice her height, and you can do the same, but the last thing you want is to look like the diminutive woman. High heels do not just give you height, they also make you walk more confidently, and it becomes easier to assume an authoritative posture."

Rachele reluctantly accepted the idea of shoe shopping with Countess Deborah the following morning. Once they had sorted the shoes, choosing clothes was less problematic. As they walked towards the dining room, Rachele brought the conversation to the work the law firm would do for the countess. They stopped before joining the rest of the family for dinner. Rachele tried to prepare her honorary aunt for the worse.

"You need to be prepared for disappointment; Alex and Franco will do their best to find information. Our Canadian nephew, Carlo Mendes, worked with Displaced People until he returned to civilian life; he may point them to alternative routes that the Red Cross did not pursue. If they come up with nothing, you must be prepared for the long and drawn process of declaring Raffaele, Sylvia, and their daughter legally dead."

The countess felt even more confident that she had summoned her 'legal cavalry.'

"I think I am rationally aware of that; I am not sure I am ready emotionally. As you know, I am invested in them like I am invested in all of you."

Rachele tried to lighten up the conversation.

"Were Emanuele and Gemma your match?"

The countess seized the chance to have the last word.

 "Of course they were. I am claiming the credit for you and Gabriele as well. After all, I invited him to dinner, didn't I?"

The two ladies smiled at each other and joined the rest of the family in the dining room.

Chapter Three

January 1948

Roberto and Rachele concentrated on recovering the assets listed in the very detailed wills. Mario and Paola Mendes, their nephew and niece, were two potential heirs. Searching for information about what happened to Raffaele, Sylvia, and Leah would represent a potential conflict of interests.

Rachele wanted to check every evidence of ownership before they petitioned to recover the assets listed in the wills on behalf of the estate. Alex Modiano wanted to finish compiling the list of what he had found before his aunt arrived from Rome later that day.

The phone he shared with Franco Cantoni was ringing. He was so focused on his task that he did not notice it until the voice of the receptionist brought him down to earth,

"Alex Modiano, pick up the blessed phone!"

It was his grandfather from Trieste. Nowadays, Baron Davide Modiano took a while to come to the point. His transition from busy entrepreneur to retired gentleman happened when he was hiding in plain sight in Venice during the final years of the war. He had time and never thought that most people in his large extended family either worked or studied and did not have all the time in the world. Alex was trying very hard to find a polite and respectful way to break the flow and ask his grandfather to come to the point when he did.

"We received a letter from your aunt in Haifa; your cousin Zvi is coming. She has written to Aunt Rachele and Uncle Gabriele because Zvi will spend most of his time in Venice. By the way, do you remember which one is Zvi? After over twenty years, I still have problems remembering the names they took when they made *aliyah*[1]."

"If I remember correctly, Zvi used to be called Conrad when they lived in Trieste. He is the same age as my sister, Paola."

"Thank you. Conrad, sorry, Zvi, wants to start a coffee roasting business in Haifa. He will spend some time with your father, but Venice will be his primary base. Your aunt Greta, I mean Ruth, tells me he has information about second-hand equipment from Vienna and Prague and wants to inspect it. Can you please ask your aunt to call me when she arrives back from Rome? I called Anita, but she told me Rachele plans to come to the office first."

Baron Modiano started enquiring about his grandson's life and work, giving Alex the perfect excuse to stop the conversation. He had something to finish before his boss, Aunt Rachele, arrived from Rome.

"Grandpa, I am sorry. I need to finish something before General Radetzky arrives from Rome."

"Do you still use that nickname for your aunt Rachele?"

"Yes, and it is well-earned. She is a caring but demanding boss. Hug Grandma Esther for me. I really need to go. Telephone hugs to you as well."

"Bless you Alex, please give my love to all the family in Venice."

Alex hung up and returned to his list of assets. He had a nagging thought that there was another reason behind his cousin Zvi's trip.

Franco Cantoni was working out of his father's office because he could not risk Alex Modiano seeing what he was doing, since Alex had a family connection with two potential heirs. His task was to find information about Raffaele Mustaki, his wife Sylvia Schwartz Mustaki, and their daughter Leah. He had contacted the organisations helping displaced people and camp survivors that Carlo Mendes had suggested and was now studying the list of people detained in a transit camp using ledgers his father had borrowed. Those ledgers represented several 'There, but for the Grace of God go I...' moments Franco was not keen to remember. He and his family hid in Asolo, a town at the foot of the Dolomites..

There was a time when Rachele would have thought of a long train journey by herself as a relaxing experience. Most of her children had grown up, and she was the boss of her law firm; long train journeys had become a waste of time. The overnight trains were no use to her. She tried it once and kept waking up each time the train stopped at a station, and there were many stations between Rome and Venice. In the past few months, she had become a frequent visitor to the airport at the Lido. Usually, Gabriele would meet her, and they would take a water taxi. This time, he was busy with one of the few clients of his bookkeeping practice, Count Contarini. Alex wanted his aunt's undivided attention to discuss a few items on the asset list. He thought that the time on the water taxi would be the perfect opportunity to talk to his aunt, with nobody else interrupting. When the flight from Rome was announced, he moved to the windows to watch the plane land and the passengers walk to the terminal. His aunt was one of a handful of women in what looked like a full flight and the only one who did not have a male travelling companion. When Rachele saw Alex, she was concerned something had happened, but she smiled when he told her why he had come. They discussed the list on the way to the office. Alex was wondering what to do with two properties in the part of Istria that the allied had handed over to Yugoslavia. Sylvia had inherited them from their father. There were other items on his list where he needed advice on what evidence was required to prove that they belonged to Raffaele or Sylvia when they were seized. When the water taxi reached Riva De Biasio, he had all the answers he needed, but there was something else he wanted to ask his aunt.

"Grandpa Davide rang me earlier to tell me that Zvi Treves will arrive in Venice."

The driver of the water taxi placed Rachele's luggage on the Riva. She paid him and waited for the boat to sail away before turning to her nephew.

"When I spoke to Gabriele this morning, he mentioned it."

"Did uncle Gabriele explain to you why Zvi is coming?"

"He did. There must be another reason for his trip. Why didn't he apply for a multi-entry visa for Trieste[2], and why is he coming here instead?"

"I had been wondering the same thing, but I thought I had better keep my doubts to myself."

"Gabriele and I used the same words this morning; let us keep our doubts to the three of us."

Alex picked up his aunt's suitcase. As they were climbing the stairs that led to the office, Rachele told him that Zvi would stay at Fiamma's home. They would organise a bed in the room they used as the law firm office before the move. Once they were inside, people started demanding Rachele's attention.

It took a while for Rachele to go from the receptionist's desk to her office. She sat down to write a letter to her sister in Israel. Roberto came in to ask her opinion on a contract. He had barely sat down when she noticed Franco Cantoni walk past; she asked him to come into her office for a few minutes.

"I am writing a letter to my sister Ruth in Haifa. She might know organisations that have information on survivors of the camps or have recovered any German documentation about former camp inmates. I told her it will help you in your search and explained why she must contact you with the answer."

Franco was holding one of the ledgers he had been working with

"I was about to ask Pina if she knew when Roberto was available. I can place Raffaele Mustaki at the Fossoli transit camp in January 1944; there seems to be no trace of his wife and daughter. I am going back to the Red Cross for more information, but so far, I only know that he left the transit camp for Dachau. It is progress. Do we tell the countess?"

Rachele stared at nothing for a few minutes. Her father-in-law spent time in the same transit camp before being transported. Then she shook her head and looked at Franco.

"I think this is something to share with her. In two months, we have achieved something she did not achieve in two years. It will reassure her she did the right thing coming to us, although we still do not know what happened to him once he was in Dachau. Her golden boy will make the call."

Roberto said he would call his honorary aunt later, but he would also tell her not to discuss it with his mother; she did not need any reminder of her husband's death. Franco also suggested organising a meeting with the countess to have information about the Schwartz family. There was a lot they did not know about Sylvia Schwartz's family, and they did not have enough information to decide who had any right to the combined estates. Roberto agreed it was a great excuse to contact his honorary aunt. They would deliver the news about Raffaele Mustaki in person.

Gabriele and Rachele were used to making time to spend alone. They enjoyed each other's company but had a large family and were running busy lives. The morning after Rachele returned from Rome was one of those clear sunny days in January. They took a walk to the end of the Cannareggio Canal to see if the day was clear enough to see the snowed peaks of the Alps.

Rachele had declined to be a candidate in the forthcoming elections, the first political elections after the Fascist dictatorship and the end of World War II. Gabriele thought he could somehow make his wife change her mind, although he knew it would not be easy.

"I thought you would seize the opportunity to be a candidate. It is the first time women vote for the national parliament. There should be more women candidates."

Whenever she wanted to make an important point, Rachele stopped walking and concentrated on her husband.

"What I do in Rome is important for Italian women and for the law firm. I help a group of politicians who want to change the Fascist family law and make some standard practices illegal.

Gabriele did not stop trying

"Think how much you can help Italian women if you are a candidate."

Rachele looked at her husband and decided she could walk and talk.

"I can make a difference as a legal advisor to a group of candidates from three parties rather than be a candidate. It also puts me in position to make several important connections that might be useful to the law firm in the long run. Also, spending most of my week in Rome is not part of my plans for the next few years."

They had reached the end of Canal Cannareggio. There was no cloud in the sky; it was a clear day, and they could definitely see the white peaks of the mountains. They stood there for about ten minutes, admiring the view in silence, just enjoying being next to each other. Gabriele put an arm around Rachele's shoulders. They turned back and started walking towards the vaporetto stop that would take them to the other side of the Grand Canal and back to their office.

A week later, Countess Pesaro De Bonfili was sitting at the head of the table in the Canal Grande meeting room for an update. Franco would spend time with her after the meeting to see if they could build a family tree of the Schwartz family; Roberto and Rachele had provided all the information about the Mustaki side. They could start filing petitions with the relevant courts to recover seized assets or seek compensation for those that had been sold and could not be recovered. They still had to find out what to do with some properties Sylvia had inherited from her father in Abbazia, now Opatija, in Istria. A territory that used to be part of Italy until the end of the war and now was part of Yugoslavia. The countess listened, took notes, and smiled a lot. Roberto braced himself for the news he had to deliver before handing the meeting over to Franco.

"Franco Cantoni had found Raffaele Mustaki in the list of people detained in the Fossoli transit camp and Dachau was his final destination, but we do not know yet what happened to him there. Franco has also made progress in finding other sources of information."

The smile had gone from the countess's face, and Rachele felt the unusual urge to hug her, but Deborah Camerini recovered relatively quickly; she turned directly to Franco.

"Franco, did you find his wife or daughter in the same camp?"

"I double-checked both under Mustaki and Schwartz. They must have been arrested at different times and sent to different places. Carlo Mendes used to take care of Displaced People in 1945 and 1946 before he went back to Canada. I wrote to him for advice, and he sent me the names of a few organisations that took care of Displaced People and contact names. I have contacted them and the Red Cross again now that we have news of Raffaele Mustaki. Also, Rachele wrote to her sister in Haifa, asking her to find out about similar organisations in Israel. I have every confidence that we shall be able to find out what happened to Raffaele's wife and daughter."

The countess could not resist the attention of a young man, even if they were not personal, so her face relaxed.

"I was right. You are the legal cavalry, and I should have come to you sooner. Now, if there is nothing else, I think I need to spend time with Franco, telling him what I know of the Schwartz family."

She stood up. The meeting was over, at least as far as she was concerned.

Chapter Four

February - March 1948

The law firm had presented the first petition to the court to recover seized assets on behalf of the executor of the wills of Raffaele Mustaki and Sylvia Schwartz. The judge had congratulated the firm for the exhaustive supportive evidence. Alvise, Rachele, and Roberto congratulated Alex Modiano for all the work he did to put the petition together; he was very proud of himself. The list of assets included in the first petition was not exhaustive; there was still more work to do, but, for the moment, he enjoyed being congratulated. They were still in a party mood when a porter delivered the luggage for Rachele's trip to Rome, and the postman delivered the mail. A letter from Trieste dampened the atmosphere; the lawyer recommended by Michele Modiano, Rachele's brother and Alex's father, had replied; it was a mixed bag. The allied administration of the free territory of Trieste had a backlog of local cases. The petition on behalf of the Mustaki-Schwartz estate had a very low priority. Although Sylvia Schwarz and her brother were born in the part of Istria that had become Yugoslavian territory, which made them 'local' to Trieste, the petition included assets on the wrong side of the border. It would be better if those assets were in a separate petition. The one concerning assets in the free territory of Trieste had more chances to be heard in good time.

Rachele had to leave for the airport. She asked Alex to help her with the suitcase. Once they were in the Riva, she spoke in a low voice.

"Zvi arrives today. Anita told me that Fiamma was in a good mood this morning, which is great. He'll sleep in the old warehouse on the ground floor, the door opposite your room."

"Do you mean the room that used to be the law firm's office?"

"Yes, that one. Could you try to find out more about his trip? Be discrete and use the family connection. After all, you have not seen him in twelve years, and no one has seen him since 1936 when they were in Italy for Grandma Esther's seventieth birthday!"

The conspiratorial tone brought a smile to Alex's face.

"I have already thought of that. Depending on how things go today, I will suggest we go out tonight or tomorrow night. After all, the official story is that he wants to follow the family tradition of dealing with coffee; you and I have broken away from it. Plenty of things to discuss."

"Great, here is the taxi. I have faith in you; we need to go out for a meal when I am back. By we, I mean you, Gabriele, and I. Meanwhile, let's keep our doubts to the three of us."

She kissed him on the cheek; Alex passed her suitcase to the driver. Rachele boarded the water taxi and was off to the airport to fly to Rome.

There were several reasons Rachele was flying rather than taking the train, the typical option for most people. Time was only one of them. She loved watching Venice from the plane during take-off. The view was incredible even on this dull day in February. As she was looking at 'La Serenissima' (the most serene city)[1], she decided that the best gift for her husband's next birthday was flying over Venice, maybe organise some days in Rome just the two of them.

Alex Modiano had arranged to meet Zvi Treves at the station. The last time they met, Italy had no racial laws, and World War II had not started. It felt like another century. Waiting for the train to arrive, Alex wondered how a 36-year-old would match his distant memory of a 24-year-old, very exotic cousin. Back then, Zvi, or Conrad as their grandparents called him, stood out from the elegant crowd celebrating their grandmother's birthday and their new cousin's brit millah[2]. His clothes could have been described as functional rather than stylish. He looked like a red-headed version of their uncle Daniele, sharing the same pale blue eyes. When the train arrived, he thought he had identified him from a distance, except he was now looking at an elegant, tall man. Alex held a sign with his cousin's name just in case they could not recognise each other. When the tall elegant red-haired man reached the end of the platform, he took the sign off Alex's hands, and hugged him. When Zvi Treves spoke, his lack of accent surprised Alex. They started walking towards Fondamenta del Ghetto. The conversation flowed as if they had not seen each other for twelve days rather than twelve years. They were discussing family; there was much to discuss, including those who had died. Alex did not expect to hear two of his cousins had fought in the Royal Air Force. Zvi did not expect to hear how many of his relatives had fought in the resistance. After they crossed Ponte delle Guglie, Alex stopped.

"I need to warn you not to discuss World War II anywhere near Fiamma. Her husband died on the train that was taking him to the camps. She was lucky enough to escape arrest; she was not home. Now, she suddenly falls silent and looks at you, but she sees her memories; then, she bursts into tears. We try not to mention the War in her presence."

They continued in silence until they walked past the Spanish synagogue. When they crossed the bridge to the Campo del Ghetto Novo, Zvi shook himself out of his thoughts.

"In the past two years, I have met other Holocaust survivors. They all share that stare into their memories when they suddenly fall silent. It is heart-breaking. So, who else lives with Uncle Gabriele's mother?"

"For the moment, just Roberto Mendes and his wife, Dina. I said for the moment, because Dina will have a baby in May; Roberto is also one of my bosses."

They had now arrived in the big house by the canal in Fondamenta del Ghetto, nothing grand, the functional home of a merchant.

The previous three evenings had been a 'whirlwind of cousins.' It did not matter whether they were Modiano cousins or members of the Mendes family and, therefore, not related to Zvi. After the war, most Italian Jews had extended the concept of family beyond people sharing a bloodline. Obviously, Countess Deborah had to inspect the 'new' young man.

Alex and Zvi were having a drink in a café in Rio Terà Frasetti, before going to Gabriele and Rachele for dinner. The conversation on the way to the café was very light-hearted.

"So, Alex, what is the connection between Countess Deborah and our family?"

"Her husband had some business connection with our grandfather, and, over time, they had become close friends. Also, the countess is a very close friend of Fiamma since they were in the same class in primary school. Our grandfather believed that aunt Rachele could have been a suitable match for Countess Deborah's son. Unfortunately, uncle Gabriele was invited to the same dinner, and the rest is history."

Zvi kept the conversation about family and away from himself. Once they entered the café, Alex noticed Zvi had chosen a table where he could check everybody's coming and going; his time in the resistance made him wonder whether Zvi's need to control his environment was a leftover of his time in the British special forces during the war or there was a reason related to why he was in Venice.

Alex had given up any hope of seamlessly moving the subject toward him and his plans. Time to change the subject.

"So, you have decided to enter the traditional family business, coffee. How far are you in your plans?"

That question did not surprise Zvi.

"I have a location for a warehouse with enough space to house the equipment to roast the coffee. I will use the family trading company to source the beans, and I have contacts to inspect second-hand equipment in Vienna and Prague."

"Why are you in Venice? You may have noticed that we are all happy to see you, but Trieste would have been the obvious place."

"I only have a single-entry visa for the Free Territory of Trieste. I must take at least two trips to Vienna and Prague, so Venice is easier. Tomorrow, I need to go to the station to buy a ticket to Vienna. It is a business trip and a trip down memory lane; I am visiting cities where I have not been in a long time."

Alex noticed that his cousin had changed position twice as he talked, a clear sign of being nervous. Zvi was careful only to say what he felt he could share, but there was a lot he could not share. Time to drop the subject before picking it up again.

"Anything that happened before the war feels far away in time. Three years ago, almost everybody you met since you arrived used false identities to escape arrest and deportation, and a lot were actively fighting against German occupations. Now, we may all carry our nightmares inside, but our lives have some semblance of normality."

Zvi strangely relaxed, as if he felt he could speak freely about the subject with no fear of revealing secrets.

"Well, this may be true here. At home, we fear war will start again, the British Mandate will end in a few months, and then trouble starts. I do not know whether you followed things, but we depend on a vote at the United Nations. We have no idea what may happen. So far, most Arab countries are opposing the partition. There is a sense of impending war. My parents are postponing their retirements, although my mother will reduce the number of hours she spends in the operating theatre."

Alex realised Zvi had unexpectedly served him the opportunity to ask what he wanted to ask. He had to be careful and not direct.

"How are your parents? I always felt I was the only person I know who could say 'my aunt, the surgeon'"

Zvi did not seem to have realised that Alex was steering the conversation in another direction. He smiled.

"I know what you mean. Back home, we may have women who fight alongside men, but there are few people who can say 'my aunt the lawyer', or 'my aunt the head of a hospital lab,' or 'my aunt the head of finance,' not to mention 'my mother the surgeon.' The Modiano women are quite something."

In his head, Alex was jumping up and down. The opportunity had arrived!

"Well, you forgot 'our aunt, the head of production,' Aunt Celeste is the one in charge of warehousing and roasting operation for the family coffee trading business. My father mostly deals with clients and suppliers overseas. Speaking of Aunt Celeste, have you thought of checking with her if they have good equipment they are replacing?"

Alex had kept a steady voice, and the question seemed plausible. Zvi did not seem to show any nervousness, and he probably had already prepared his answer to a question he must have expected that some family member would ask.

"I had this conversation with my mother several times. The allied administration of the territory is cautious with any equipment export; they are concerned that companies may want to relocate to escape a touchy political environment."

The answer did not convince Alex, but their aunt and uncle had invited them to dinner. Alex thought they could not be late; he did not want to risk Anita's wrath if they were late for dinner. They stood up, paid, and left the café. Later, Zvi had a problem keeping a straight face when they placed him near the countess.

The three partners of the Modiano-Mendes-Cantoni law firm met over coffee in Rachele's office. The grey and foggy winter day meant they had the light turned on. Rachele could not understand why, but she felt as if they were three co-conspirators in some plot rather than three partners discussing their legal practice. Rachele's time in Rome allowed the firm to bid for a complex unravelling of contracts allegedly signed under duress. The client was based in Milan, but their combined expertise gave them a very good chance. Rachele closed the 'Rome' folder and opened another called 'Venice'. It was Roberto's turn to report.

"Thanks to Alex, we have filed most petitions to recover all properties seized from Raffaele Mustaki. We need to decide who goes to Milan to file the rest. We have a few problems with Sylvia Schwartz. Her brother wrote to us from Boston, Zia Deborah contacted him. When their mother died in 1938, they thought that having everything in his name would save the assets. After all, he was a citizen of the United States living in Boston. They did not consider the war. We are waiting for Guido Schwartz to instruct us to recover the assets seized when Italy declared war on the United States."

Rachele stopped taking notes

"It is a different process. So far, we have petitioned the court in Venice and Trieste for what was in Sylvia's name. We need to discuss with Guido Schwartz whether he wants us to represent him to recover the assets that used to be in his name and have not been returned to him so far."

Roberto nodded and wrote a note to write to Guido Schwartz to discuss recovering his assets, before continuing his report

"The court in Trieste will validate our claims on properties in what is now Yugoslavia. Their ruling may help us the day we can either petition a court in Pola or Fiume or petition the Italian state for reparations."

Alvise added that Franco had contacted all the organisations Carlo Mendes had suggested. Hopefully, one of them will answer with some relevant news.

Alex, Gabriele, and Rachele discussed Zvi Treves over lunch at a nice fish restaurant on Giudecca Island. They had not figured out why he was in Venice. They would reconvene in a month and see if they had made any progress; Zvi was supposed to stay till at least the end of April, if not longer.

Meanwhile, they would not share their doubts with anybody else.

On their *way* back to the office, when they were almost at the Riva De Biasio stop, they changed the subject, discussing the official reason for lunch. They discussed one of Rachele's cases where Alex had put a lot of time, a private investigator had to be hired, and there were other expenses. Gabriele was supposed to write a complicated and fully itemised bill for that client. They walked into the office, still talking about the case. Franco walked towards them, showing a letter with a Swiss postmark. The agency in Geneva suggested by Carlo Mendes had replied to his letter faster than anybody had expected. Franco was so excited that he wanted to open the letter and read it aloud in front of as many people as possible. The result came after a very polite introduction.

"Based on the documentation we have collected so far, we can confirm that Sylvia Schwartz and her daughter, Leah Mustaki, were arrested in a small town on Lake Iseo in January 1944. They were deported to Birkenau, where they were separated. Sylvia died in March 1944 of tuberculosis. We have a record of a Leah Mustaki in one of the Displacement People Camps in Germany, and according to the doctors in the camp, she has memory issues. Please write to the camp management at this address for more details about her and her conditions. We also found a record of a Raffaele Mustaki who died in the Dachau's camp in February 1944 on arrival from a transit camp in Italy."

The room was silent for quite a few minutes. The first to speak was Alvise. He was the one who had never met them, so he had a less intense reaction to the news of their death.

"We are not sure whether the Leah Mustaki they have found is their daughter, but, according to the terms of Raffaele Mustaki's will, his wife would be his sole heir if he predeceased her when their daughter was still a minor. So,

Mario and Paola are not heirs because they are his sister's children. Rachele and Roberto, your conflict of interest ends here."

They decided that Roberto, Gabriele, and Rachele would pay a visit to the countess to tell her the news; it would be better than having her come to the office. Meanwhile, Franco was supposed to follow up on the lead to find Leah Mustaki and write to the address in the letter. Alvise would write to Sylvia's brother in Boston to update him and tell him he may be the heir if Leah Mustaki did not prove to be Raffaele and Sylvia's daughter.

Roberto, Gabriele, and Rachele were sitting in the small sitting room in the home of their honorary aunt. The countess apologised for the 'small intimate setting for tea,' as she had rented the large sitting room with a view of Rialto bridge to an American magazine for a fashion shoot. Roberto had asked his brother and his sister-in-law to be there to support him, and Rachele might help if the countess became too emotional. He hoped that their relationship of mutual respect and warm non-belligerence meant that Rachele could be counted on to come to the brothers' rescue in the unlikely event that Countess Pesaro de Bonfili would start crying.

They were all sitting down in navy blue armchairs with golden frames; the upholstery matched the curtains, other decorations of the room, and the countess's grey and blue dress. Rachele wondered if there was a fashion shoot in the other room or if the red damask upholstery clashed with what Aunt Deborah was wearing, but she kept her thoughts to herself.

While waiting for refreshments and biscuits, Gabriele remarked he had fond memories of that room. When the refreshments came, the countess pointed out that they all came from Anna's new kosher patisserie. Deborah Camerini was now ready to come to the point. As usual, she looked at her golden boy before talking. Gabriele and Rachele could not help but smile at her predictability.

"As happy as I am to see you, I wonder why you insisted on coming today. "

Roberto was not entirely sure how to say it tactfully. Rachele took over.

"We have received confirmation that Raffaele and Sylvia are dead. There is, however, some uncertainty about Leah."

After what everybody felt was a very long silence, Roberto explained the letter written to an agency in Geneva following a suggestion from their nephew Carlo and the content of their reply. The countess listened to her golden boy with a very serious face. Rachele was concerned; she stood up from her armchair and moved next to her honorary aunt to be ready for whatever assistance was necessary. However, they had underestimated Deborah Camerini, Countess Pesaro de Bonfili. She straightened her posture before she started talking.

"I have several thoughts about the Leah Mustaki mentioned in the letter, but I have to talk to my children first. I will come to the office as soon as possible and formally discuss her with my legal cavalry."

She then poured herself more coffee, offered more cake and biscuits to her guests, before she continued as if her honorary nephews had just come to see her socially.

"Roberto, how is your wife doing? Which room did you decide to use for the nursery? You have slightly more than a couple of months to early May. It is not a lot of time."

Chapter Five

March-April 1948

Gabriele and Rachele were drinking coffee in her office; Gabriele was leaning by the window when he noticed the countess coming off the vaporetto. She was walking with the determination she usually showed at an art auction when there was something she really wanted. She was expected, so everybody was ready. Gabriele popped out in the corridor and shouted, "She's here" and everybody reacted like soldiers who were about to be inspected by their commander-in-chief. When she rang the doorbell, everybody had checked their appearance and stood straight and ready for inspection.

Aunt Deborah waltzed in with a smile, greeted the receptionist and Rachele very warmly, and was escorted to the meeting room, where she fawned over her cavalry, Gabriele, Roberto, Alex, and Franco. Alvise was the last one to appear; this time, he remembered to kiss her hand rather than shake it, she was genuinely surprised he remembered. Alvise looked like the cat who ate the canary. Gabriele thought that Aunt Deborah's face was priceless.

Alvise gave a formal update on the situation, which included a chart with Schwartz's and Mustaki's family trees and an explanation of the line of inheritance. Rachele could tell their client was making all the right noises showing interest, but she was bored. Roberto gave her an update on the court cases to recover seized properties, but it was clear to Rachele that the countess was growing impatient. She had something to tell them and was eager to say it. Her upbringing forced her to be patient until her turn finally came.

"I have spoken to my children, and they agree with me. We would like Alex and Franco to travel to the DP camp where the young woman that calls herself Leah Mustaki is. I know she may not be Raffaele and Sylvia's daughter, but I also know that the only way to find out is to bring her here. She will stay with me. Even if she is not the Leah Mustaki we are looking for, she is a young woman in a refugee camp, obviously without a family. She deserves a home, and I would like to see if we can give her one. So, can you please help me make it happen? By the way, I thought of Alex and Franco because I know Alex is fluent in German and English, and Franco speaks English. Franco is also familiar with the family tree of the Schwartz and Mustaki families. I will pay all their expenses, of course."

Everybody was speechless. They did not expect that. The first one to recover was Franco Cantoni. He chose not to comment on what the countess had just said, leaving the decision to his bosses, but informed her he had contacted Sylvia's brother in Boston.

Gabriele's role in the firm made him an observer. The face of his colleagues reminded him of the stunned faces of art dealers when the countess would make the surprising final bid at an art auction and get the piece they all wanted.

Rachele was the first of the partners to find her voice; she simply said they would investigate it and let her know about timing and costs as soon as possible. She then excused herself, claiming she had to prepare for another meeting and went back to her office. Leaving Deborah Camerini as the queen bee of her cavalry regiment.

The countess had decided that Alex and Franco should travel in style, because they had to face long train journeys with no time to rest. She had contacted the Jewish Agency in Geneva herself, asked them to organise Alex and Franco's visit to the DP camp, and wondered if they minded briefing her two emissaries beforehand. Once she had confirmed dates, she went to a travel agency and then appeared at the headquarters of her legal cavalry with tickets, hotel reservations, and confirmed appointments. Alex and Franco were now on the train to Geneva to visit the agency that gave them information about Leah, the first leg of a week of lengthy train rides and short stays. They both described the other as 'family' without getting into details, but they were nervous at the idea of spending so much time together. Franco Cantoni had been part of the inner core of the Mendes clan from birth; his parents were close friends of Gabriele and Rachele. Alex has always been considered family because he was his aunt's nephew. However, they had never spent seven days in close proximity. They were watching the countryside from the window of their compartments, both reassured by how comfortable they felt sharing silence.

The following day they were at the agency that briefed them about their search and why there were doubts about the identity of Leah Mustaki. Her looks were irrelevant; time in a Nazi concentration camp would cause several development issues for a child facing puberty. The number tattooed on her arms did not match the record of the camp; it was unusual for a German administrative officer to make mistakes in registering prisoners. Franco mentioned that his younger sister had known Leah Mustaki, but he had the memory of an eight-year-old in 1939, not a 16-year-old. He could not trust his memory, but he could ask her questions only the real Leah Mustaki could answer. They were both informed that the young woman in question had complained of memory loss. She had developed a close relationship with the wife of the camp's rabbi, which is why they had arranged for Franco and Alex to talk to the rabbinical couple before meeting Leah.

Countess Deborah was used to doing things to her own high standards. Franco and Alex had single accommodations in sleeping compartments on the train to Germany. They were still half asleep when they changed to a regional train that took them to the small town halfway between Hamburg and Bremen, where the Displaced People camp was located. They were both uneasy being in Germany. Franco commented that the sound of the German language had spelt trouble for over a year and a half, and he had a hard time reconciling it with ordinary life in a small town. Alex refused to start any conversation in German; he stuck to English. After all, they were in the part of Germany still under the jurisdiction of the British Army. The travel agency used by Countess Deborah had arranged accommodation with the only hotel in town. Both young men were uneasy at the idea of spending four days in Germany, but they knew they would go back to Venice. Many people they knew did not have that certainty a few years earlier.

Things changed when they reached the Displaced People camp; it was unmistakably an old Army barrack, but the people they met were British military or American volunteers; the atmosphere was decidedly different from the village. The American rabbi and his wife expected them; they would spend the afternoon talking to them, and then Leah Mustaki would arrive for dinner. Franco Cantoni followed the Jewish dietary rules fairly strictly, so he had been on a steady diet of raw salad and boiled eggs; he could not wait for dinner at the Rabbi's home. Ruth, the Rabbi's wife, had prepared some food with the coffee. When she brought the tray into the living room, she looked at Franco's face, put the tray down, returned to the kitchen, and reappeared with another tray with lunch leftovers. The Rabbi remarked that the global conspiracy of Jewish mothers had decided that someone looked hungry. After Franco finished eating, a smile back on his face, they discussed the reason for their visit. Alex and Franco could tell that the Rabbi and his wife cared for the young woman from the tone of their voices.

"Memory loss is not uncommon among those who survived the march out of Birkenau in the war's last days. The real problem is that the number tattooed on her arm is one digit lower than the number associated with Leah Mustaki in the camp register. Her number matches a name that is written one line above Leah's."

Franco understood, but not completely

"Couldn't it just be an understandable mistake?"

"The two girls were used for medical experiments; usually records were accurately kept in that environment. It is possible that they were assigned to the hospital after they tattooed the numbers, but given their experiments somewhere somehow, there would have been a note of the previous mistake. That created a few problems when she was unconscious in the hospital. They could not be sure what experiments they used her for."

Ruth Lazar added

"I think there is no family left, therefore she is still here after more than two years from the end of the war. She is too young to receive an immigrant visa on her own. Somehow, she never considered moving to the Holy Land. We were advised not to mention the other name until she gives any sign of recovering her memory."

She then stood up, in her opinion Alex and Franco still looked hungry. When she was in the kitchen, Rav Lazar added

"We know her mother died, whatever her name is. We can only assume her father died. She has now started working with a British doctor to see if she can remember anything before she woke up in the hospital, after several days of light coma. "

He turned to Franco

"I am happy you used to know Leah, I am intrigued to see if she reacts to your name."

Ruth Lazar came back with biscuits and hot drinks. They spent two hours discussing Leah; she arrived an hour before dinner. Alex and Franco were introduced to her as two Jewish journalists from Italy. Leah spoke English with an American accent, undoubtedly resulting from her strong relationship with the Rabbi's wife. Her reaction to Franco Cantoni was intriguing.

"Cantoni? I have vague memories of a Lisa Cantoni. We must have played together because I associate the name with a square with no cars."

Franco was surprised but not as surprised as the Rabbi and his wife. He whispered to Alex

"It is the first time she has spoken about her childhood."

Franco tried to be as matter of fact as possible

"Lisa is my sister, you probably remember the square in Venice where we used to live and still do."

"Do you know anything about my family?"

Franco and Alex looked at each other; they looked at the Rabbi's wife, who nodded. Franco answered, following what they had agreed earlier.

"I know you have an uncle in Boston, and I will contact him to tell him about you. Your parents had good friends in Venice, and somebody who knew your father since he was born has been looking for you for almost three years."

Leah became very sad; she was fighting tears. The Rabbi's wife hugged her and asked what the problem was. Leah did not answer; she just started sobbing. After a few minutes, she simply said.

"I do not remember any of it. My life before the hospital is just a big blur."

They spent more time with Leah during the Sabbath; the Rabbi insisted they move out of their hotel and stay with them. Alex and Franco were relieved to leave the German village; they were more relaxed in the Rabbi's home. They also had the opportunity to spend time with Leah, who unfortunately did not have any other recollection of her time before the camps. On the following Monday, they left for the station, telling the Rabbi that they would probably be in touch soon once they had discussed their visit with their client. The countess had decided they would love to travel back home as fast as possible after a few days in Germany. She had organized tickets to fly to Venice. Alex and Franco had been speaking English to each other during the train journey to Hamburg, including the taxi to the airport, and switched to Italian once the plane had taken off. They were relieved to leave Germany.

The countess had decided that Rachele was the best person to share her plans with. She needed to talk to somebody who could appreciate the emotional and legal sides, be discreet and not share the conversation with anybody, not even her husband or her partners. She knew Rachele could keep things to herself and invited her to have a morning coffee at a café near Rialto. They talked about family and wondered whether Alex and Franco would be nervous flying for the first time. It was a pleasant and relaxed atmosphere. Once the countess had decided that the polite part of the conversation was over, she came to the point.

"I need your opinion as a mother, my honorary niece, and the most brilliant legal mind I know. I would like to share with you what I have in mind. We are here because it is not yet a plan; it is just an idea. I have been thinking of that teenage girl alone in a refugee camp without a family. It is almost irrelevant whether she is Leah Mustaki; that is a legal matter and plays no role in what I have in mind. I could give her a family. I am in good health. If she is 16, I have no reason to think I won't be around till she turns 21. I have no intention of adopting her, more like becoming her guardian. My children agree. I want to give her a home and support her until she is ready to face the world. What do you think? How complicated might it be?"

Rachele was amazed but not completely surprised. Over the years, she had realised that her honorary aunt was very generous and prepared to go out of her way to help anybody she knew. She slowly sipped her coffee to take time before she answered.

"Let's start with the straightforward part. I think we should wait until Franco and Alex have told us what they found; then, we must establish if she really is Leah Mustaki. If she is, she has an uncle in Boston that might have your ideas, and no court would choose you over him. If she is not Leah Mustaki, she is a stateless refugee, and we need to sort her legal status in this country before we discuss guardianship."

The countess was not sipping her coffee or eating whatever was left of her cake. She was giving Rachele her undivided attention. Her honorary niece paused for effect. It was one of her tricks when she was in court whenever she wanted to emphasise the point she was about to make.

"Now, for the complicated part, are you sure? Shouldn't you wait until we have brought her here? Have her stay with you while we establish her identity. Get to know her, wait a couple of months, and then revisit this decision. If she is Leah or as old as Leah, you are about to make a five-year commitment. Just wait. Also, I would discuss it with your children before you act."

The countess could do pauses as well. She slowly sipped her coffee before speaking.

"You have a point; I shall wait. One more thing, could we keep this conversation strictly among ourselves? I thought of having regular morning coffee with you, maybe every other week; we can discuss this confidential matter away from everybody else."

Rachele agreed. The countess then changed the subject and started discussing Rachele's eldest daughter, Emma, and her husband. They were due to spend two weeks in Venice and celebrate Passover with everybody else; the whole family was thrilled. As they were parting company, it was Rachele's turn to change the subject once more. She asked the countess whether she intended to vote at the elections. That allowed the countess to have the final parting comment.

"You are the second person who reminded me today. As I said to my daughter three hours ago, I have. It is the first time Italian women can vote for the parliament; of course, I shall vote."

~

The following day, Alex and Franco were back in the office, still excited by their first two flights. They both wrote to the countess, thanking her for giving them the excitement of travelling by plane for the first time. By the end of the morning, they had probably told everybody about their first take-off from Hamburg and the excitement of flying over the Alps at least twice. Initially, people smiled. After the third time they heard the story, they were more dismissive. When the countess arrived for her meeting, they were about to start again when Alvise suggested they could take her out to lunch, if she were available, to thank her and tell her all about the excitement. Rachele whispered to her honorary aunt that they had heard the story at least three times and brought the focus of the conversation back to Leah Mustaki. Alex and Franco calmed down and shared their impressions. Franco thought she was the real Leah Mustaki, simply because she reacted to his last name and mentioned his sister, but he had doubts. Alex's suspicions mostly came from what they told him in Geneva about the mismatch between the number tattooed on her arm by the Nazi and her name in the registers. They both agreed that her memory loss was convincing.

The countess looked at Rachele before speaking. Their silent exchange and their smiles were not lost on Alvise and Roberto.

"I think the only way is to bring her here. The Rabbi and his wife seem to have developed a strong bond with her. Did you discuss the possibility of her coming to Venice with them? We should work on that; you will take care of the legal, and I will take care of the emotional part. I will contact the Rabbi and his wife and see what they think, but won't mention the inheritance, just discuss the family angle."

She opened her handbag and looked for something, her face lit up when she found her address book.

"I will also write to Guido Schwartz, or whatever name he uses in Boston, explaining that it is easier for us to establish whether she is his niece here in Venice. You figure out the legal implications. Can we please keep the costs of this separate from the estate? I will pay for it. Last but not least, can somebody give me Rav Lazar's address?"

She then looked at Rachele and nodded. Once again, the exchange was not lost on Alvise and Roberto. Roberto wondered whether the warm non-belligerence had turned into complicity; maybe they would have to run for the metaphorical hills if that was the case.

After lunch with Aunt Deborah, Alex and Franco went home. They had to study, they both had to catch up after spending more than a week travelling around Europe. Alex noticed that his cousin Zvi was packing. He was leaving for Trieste the following day to see their grandparents and the rest of the family. He had finally obtained a multi-entry visa for the Free Territory of Trieste. The first roasting machine from Prague was supposed to arrive in Trieste the following week for transhipment to Haifa, and he had to ensure that all the parts were included in the shipment. Alex thought his cousin had come back from Vienna while they were away; maybe he had been to Prague from there. He also wondered whether the crates really contained parts of a roasting machine or something else. He kept his thoughts to himself.

Chapter Six

April-May 1948

Gabriele and Rachele were over the moon; they would celebrate Passover with all their children. Emma, their eldest daughter, and her husband Roberto Sonnino were due to arrive from Venezuela, where they lived because of Roberto's job with an oil company. The sun was shining, and the temperature was just right; the beautiful spring morning further enhanced their mood.

They seldom discussed work while walking together, but aunt Deborah and Leah Mustaki were a grey area. They were clients of the law firm, but they were also family. Leah was due to arrive in Venice after Passover; they had arranged an urgent resident permit for a stateless person who was listed as a refugee. The law firm received a temporary two-year visa quickly because Leah Mustaki could be an Italian citizen once her identity was confirmed. Rachele knew the name that matched Leah's tattooed number in the register of Birkenau camp, but she did not tell anybody. She wanted to meet the girl and figure out whether she had really lost her memory.

When they arrived at the office, the receptionist gave Rachele three letters. One from the Rabbi in the Displaced People camp, one from Boston, and the third from a professional contact in Rome. Rachele put the letter from the Rabbi in her handbag; she would discuss it during her next coffee session with the countess, set aside the letter from Boston for the forthcoming partners' meeting and opened the letter from Rome. She smiled when she read that the group of politicians and lawyers campaigning for changes to women's rights in Italy would continue to meet irrespective of the election outcome.

Rachele and the countess were having coffee in St Mark's Square. People had started travelling again. They could talk in a café surrounded by tourists and be sure those sitting near them could not understand a word they were saying. They were comparing the letters they had received from the Rabbi. The countess was looking forward to Leah's arrival; her father had been one of her honorary nephews. Leah was part of her family.

"The Rabbi and his wife are travelling with Leah. They will leave the Sunday after Passover, spend a week in Venice to help Leah get acquainted with her new environment, and then return to Germany. I will now organise their tickets. I want them to travel in comfort. Yesterday, I made a very nice profit at an art auction, and I will use that money to make them travel in style."

Rachele had to smile; she had warned the countess not to get too attached to the young girl who may not end up being the Leah Mustaki they were looking for. She decided not to repeat her warning.

"In the letter he wrote me, he confirmed he had received the paperwork to show at the Italian border so they can stamp the papers the camp administration has provided to Leah. He also has a copy of the letter the agency in Geneva wrote us authenticated by the court, including the doubt about her identity and the name associated with the number the Nazis tattooed on her forearm when she arrived at Birkenau."

Rachele's tone of voice became mellower. She put the paperwork she was holding back in her briefcase before continuing. The Jewish mother's voice had replaced the lawyer's voice.

"I hope for the young woman's sake that spending time in Venice will bring her memory back."

The countess had a pensive look but forced herself to smile before talking.

"I hope I shall establish a bond with her. Leah or no Leah, I want to help her rebuild herself and help prepare for her future. I was lucky; my children were lucky, and almost all my honorary nephews and nieces were lucky."

Memories of people who had not been lucky came flooding her mind. She started at nothing for a short time before continuing.

"Well, all except Emanuele, Gemma, and Leah's parents, who are no longer with us. Whoever she is, I want to help her in memory of those who were not lucky enough to escape deportation and the camps."

Certain things never change. It was the third time after the war that the Mendes family and extended clan were celebrating Passover. People had changed, nothing else. The extended family was going to what was now Roberto's home for lunch; they were walking in small groups. Zvi Treves was talking to Emma's husband, Roberto Sonnino; he wanted to get to know his new cousin. Alex was catching up with his cousin, Emma. They had crossed the bridge into the Ghetto Novo when Emma changed the subject.

"Alex, you live with Zvi in Grandma Fiamma's home. Have you figured out what he is doing here? His story does not add up. Maybe my experience during the war makes me weary, but somehow, I do not think he is just setting up a coffee roasting company in Haifa. I find it strange to believe he is leaving for Prague in two days; coffee roasting is not that urgent."

Alex took his time to answer. When he was ready to speak, they were about to cross the bridge into Fondamenta del Ghetto, and he knew the archway would have amplified his voice, so he waited until they had crossed the small bridge.

"I have had my doubts since he arrived. I know your parents have their doubts as well. We sort of agreed not to discuss them. Just between the two of us, I do not believe the coffee roasting story. Maybe it is what I did during the war, but some of his answers sound vague. I hope that what he does is not illegal. I suspect your mother prefers not to know. "

"My mother has always been great at plausible deniability."

They had arrived at the Mendes family home; the small groups were merging into a large one. Emma and Alex changed the subject and started talking about the synagogue service while joining the others.

The countess and Franco Cantoni were at the station waiting for the train bringing Leah and her two travelling companions to Venice. Franco was there because he had met them before, and the countess hoped he would have been a familiar face and a reassuring presence for Leah. He would also recognise the Rabbi and his wife, which would have made meeting them more personal than simply showing up with a sign with their names written on it. Deborah Camerini was apprehensive. She had not seen Leah in seven years; several things happened during those years: war, deportation, and puberty. Leah or no Leah, she hoped she could help the young woman move on from her nightmares. She was sure the young woman had nightmares. Hopefully, they would bond. Technically, she might be her temporary guardian, but the age gap was such she could be her grandmother, although she would never have admitted it.

A middle-aged couple with a teenage girl were walking toward Franco, smiling. The countess had no doubts they were Leah and her travelling companions. Franco introduced them, the Rabbi thanked her for first-class tickets; they had been unnecessary, but they enjoyed the extra comfort and their sleeping accommodation. The Rabbi spoke English and talked to Franco, expecting him to translate what he had just said. The countess surprised him when she replied in heavily accented but understandable English.

Other people noticed Leah's arrival. A blond man in his fifties and a younger man in his late twenties were waiting for the train from Trieste. The blond man had noticed the countess, who had taken even greater care in her appearance than usual. He and his companion were looking at her when the Rabbi and Leah emerged from the crowd that had just arrived. The blond man recognised Leah, a blast from the past. He did not know who her travelling companions, the elderly, but still very good-looking, lady and the young man who met them were. The young woman could recognise him, and that was a problem. He whispered to his companion that he had just seen a ghost, except she was alive and very well. He wondered how she could have survived.

Franco and the countess had agreed to take a longer route; Franco wanted to verify Leah's memory of playing with his sister by walking across the campo where they used to play.

Her reaction to Venice was interesting. They had crossed the Ponte degli Scalzi over the Grand Canal. They did not have to, but Franco wanted to check Leah's reaction to the Rialto bridge. A bridge she would have had to cross to go to a play date with his sister. They used to live on the opposite side of the Grand Canal. When they reached the bridge, Leah did not disappoint. She slowed down.

"This looks very familiar. Is the shop selling necklaces made of glass still there?"

The countess looked at Franco, then whispered to Ruth Lazar,

"Before the war, there was a shop selling necklaces and other glass objects made in Murano."

She then added with a louder voice,

"Unfortunately not. The owner's wife died, and he sold everything and moved away to live with his sister."

Leah smiled and adjusted her posture, standing taller. She was happy she remembered something. They arrived at Countess Pesaro De Bonfili's home. The staircase impressed the Rabbi and his wife, but it became obvious they had seen nothing yet. Once they entered her flat, and saw the art on the walls, they said more than once that they felt they were in a museum. Leah surprised everybody.

"Could I have been here before? I remember a room with blue and gold armchairs. I could be wrong. It is a sort of photograph that I thought of just now."

The countess and Franco smiled at each other, and the countess opened a door

"You were here several times before the war. If you look inside that room, you will see armchairs upholstered in navy blue velvet with the wooden frame painted gold."

~

The law firm had received another letter from Boston; Guido Schwartz was now using the name Gary. He informed them that his son, Joshua, was stationed in Austria and about to end his time with the military. He had written to him asking him to go to Venice instead of going back to the US, so they should hear from his son in early May. A few days later, they received a letter announcing his arrival in Venice and that he had booked a room near Piazzale Roma. He also added that he had very few memories of Venice from his childhood, so he hoped that the location of his room would be convenient for the law firm. He had booked it until the end of September.

The countess and Rachele were having one of their regular coffee-chat. Sitting in a café in Santa Croce, they looked like the other middle-class ladies gracing the establishment at that time of the day, except they were a lawyer and an art dealer, something as unusual in the late forties as it had been before the war. Rachele was using every trick she learned during her time in the Resistance to ensure they could have a confidential conversation without being overheard. They were at a corner table at the far end of the café, far from the door and other tables. Rachele had used the excuse of not being dressed warm enough for the weather. Outside, it was windy. A lot of ladies were wearing lightweight coats; Rachele was not.

Once the waiter brought in coffee and the pastries they had ordered, the countess came to the point.

"Leah has settled in quite well; there are days when she recognises a place, and they are great days! Walking around Venice with her is intriguing; it is almost as if she recognised places she read about; sometimes, she adds personal details that only the real Leah could know. I wonder if I should get professional help from somebody."

Rachele and Gabriele had met Leah without their children. They thought that meeting Mario and Paola, her cousins, could wait till Leah felt more settled; after all, she had been in Venice without the Rabbi and his wife less than a week.

"I think her memory issues are genuine, maybe because she does not want to remember something that happened at Birkenau. I have seen her records. They performed medical experiments on her, and she was in the so-called *death march*. Apparently, when the Russian army was approaching Auschwitz/Birkenau, they made them walk for days without food. Many people died. It is a miracle she made it. I guess there is a lot she'd rather not remember."

The countess put down her cup of coffee.

"Do you see why I want to help her, whoever she is? I was lucky my housekeeper kept my secret for more than a year and a half. Also, my children were lucky because they had the means to bribe people and made it to Switzerland. Emanuele and Gemma were not that lucky; Raffaele and Sylvia were not that lucky; Leah or no, Leah, she was not lucky either. I suspect that being a human guinea pig saved her, whatever they did to her. She deserves better."

The countess picked up the cup again, sipped some coffee before continuing

"Back to the inheritance. I understand Giosuè, I mean Joshua Schwartz will arrive in Venice next week."

Rachele was happy her honorary aunt changed the subject. She was not keen to remember the war; she did not like thinking of the many narrow escapes she and her family had.

"Yes, he has written directly to the law firm. He has booked accommodation till September."

"I haven't seen him since they moved to the United States twelve years ago. I do not think I'll be able to recognise him."

Rachele reached for the small glass of water that came with her coffee.

"Guido Schwartz wrote he has his power of attorney for the inheritance and another one to take Leah to the United States if we are certain she is Leah Mustaki. I am not sure we shall be able to establish her identity with no doubt between now and the end of September."

"Is there anything we can do to prove her identity beyond waiting for her memory to come back?"

"We could investigate the other name, the one I am not telling you because I do not want to influence you. The camp records show where the person with that name came from; maybe there is somebody left there who remembers her and could recognise her. By the way, she would be an Italian citizen, anyway."

The countess was intrigued and tried to see if she could get more out of Rachele.

"Remind me why you do not tell me the other possible identity of that troubled young woman."

Rachele smiled; she expected that question.

"You live with her, walk around Venice with her, talk about her past and her family. I have spoken to the doctor helping Paola; she thinks it is better if you don't know the other identity because you will have no preconceived notion. You said you want to help her, whether or not she is Leah. At the moment, the best way to help her is to give her a sense of family and a safe environment. She had it with the Rabbi and his wife; now, she needs to build it with you. "

The countess was checking her makeup, her usual move when she wanted to buy time before answering.

"I understand. I am not sure I like it, but I understand. By the way, how's Paola?"

"She is improving. She still has bad days, gets very shy when somebody wearing a uniform comes near her, and has mixed feelings about seeing the lady who took in her and her brother half an hour before her parents got arrested. Interestingly, Mario does not have his sister's issues, yet they have been through the same thing."

The countess stared at her memories for a moment; Emanuele and Gemma, Mario and Paola's parents, were shot when they tried to escape from where they were taken after being arrested in December 1943.

"Maybe because he stayed away from the window and did not see his parents being taken away. Anyway, when do you think we can organise a meeting between them?"

"Let's wait till the baby is born, and then you and Leah can come to Fiamma for lunch. Everybody will be in neutral territory. Fiamma already offered."

It was the morning after a big family dinner, and everybody was there: children, grownups, and close friends. They were celebrating the birth of the state of Israel and the Brit Millah[1] of the latest addition to the Mendes clan, Silvio Mendes, born eight days earlier. The first birth in the family after World War II. Rachele and Gabriele had discussed Mario, Paola, and Leah during the walk to the office. They were late, but still euphoric. When they arrived, the receptionist greeted them, handed over the mail, and told them that Joshua Schwartz had arrived and was waiting in the Canal Grande meeting room. He had declined the coffee she had offered him.

Rachele wondered what language to use with him. He was twelve when he left Italy; he had been stationed in Vienna for three years as part of the US army forces and might have decent German. They had at least two languages in common.

She might have met the child a few times, but had no memory of spending any time with him. Other people mentioned his red hair and green eyes, saying that they came from his mother, the daughter of Ukrainian Jews who had arrived in Venice in the late 1800s on their way to America but never crossed the Atlantic. Joshua Schwartz was standing by the window, looking outside. Rachele could tell that the red hair was still there. The child had grown into a tall young man. She coughed, and he turned around; the grey eyes were still there. Rachele tried Italian

"I must apologise, but we celebrated last night's big news and my latest nephew's Brit Millah. We did not expect you till lunchtime; my partners Roberto Mendes and Alvise Cantoni will come in an hour."

Joshua replied in heavily accented Italian.

"It does not matter. I arrived last night on a daytime train. It was my first time crossing the Alps. The views were magnificent. I'll come back around 2 pm."

He left just when Alex Modiano came in with Zvi Treves. Zvi and Joshua looked at each other as if they both tried to place the other; they shook their heads and continued walking. Rachele noticed it. She explained who that person was and asked Zvi if he had met him before. Zvi was vague as usual; he looked familiar but could not place him. Maybe he just reminded him of another red-haired man.

They were ready for Joshua Schwartz when he came back at 2 pm. The others member of his legal team introduced themselves and gave him an update on the situation. Halfway through the meeting, Rachele asked if he preferred using English or German. She could brief him in German, and Alex and Franco could brief him in English. Joshua mentioned maybe he could use the translation of some of the legal terms, but his Italian was good enough to have a general idea of the situation. He also said that he does not remember his cousin Leah, who was six when his family left for the United States, so he could not help them establish her identity. He asked for a detailed summary of all the estate assets; they told him that Alex would compile a list, including an overview of the various petitions to reclaim them. Joshua seemed disappointed to find out it would take months, if not years, to recover everything and sort them out. He looked even more disappointed when they told him that cash was frozen until the court had decided on restitution, and there was no point in trying to sell anything. He left his address with them and agreed to have an update twice a month or whenever there was something meaningful to report. In the meantime, he would get re-acquainted with Venice and maybe travel around Italy. He had not been back since the family left in 1936.

Alex Modiano had agreed to take Fiamma to Piazza San Marco for a concert by the city band; towards the end, they were surprised to realise that there was a very high tide, 'acqua alta' rarely happens at the end of May. San Marco is one of the low points of Venice; the water had just flooded the square, enough to wet the shoes of those sitting listening to the concert. Nobody moved; the water was not very high. The soles of Alex and Fiamma's shoes were wet, but their feet felt dry. By the time the concert was over, the tide had passed its peak, so they did not foresee any trouble going home. On the vaporetto, Fiamma noticed their shoes were still wet. They got off the vaporetto at the San Marcuola stop; by the time they reached Rio Terà San Leonardo, they bumped into Zvi, who claimed he had been to the same concert in San Marco square and had walked home. Only when Alex was in bed waiting for sleep did he remember that Zvi's shoes were not wet. When they got to a narrow Calle before Fondamenta del Ghetto, he stepped behind Fiamma and Zvi; her shoes were still wet, and his shoes were not. Where had Zvi been? Why did he lie?

~

Aunt Deborah, as she insisted on being called by Leah, had decided that her honorary great-niece needed a summer wardrobe. She had dragged Leah away from the armchair in the study, where she loved to spend time reading. They were now on their way to the Giudecca. Mrs Toffolo had been Emma Mendes's former employer, which is why Countess Deborah tried her out; the quality of the work coming from her workshop had been enough to turn her and the whole Mendes clan into regular clients. Leah was both excited and wary of the vaporetto. She had taken to standing like a true Venetian, but was not yet rushing in and out as a true local. They reached a stop. Leah was trying to get out of the way of people gathering to get off. Aunt Deborah had told her it was not their stop yet. Suddenly, she felt a hand push her and another grab her to prevent her from falling overboard. The countess wondered why the person who pushed her was in such a rush and thanked the crew member, who was quick to catch Leah. The young woman was shaken. An elderly gentleman gave up his seat for her. By the time they were looking at magazines and material in Mrs Toffolo's workshop, Leah seemed to have forgotten about the incident.

It was the first time that Leah had dresses made, or at least the first time she remembered. The countess decided they both deserved a treat. She took Leah for ice cream at the Zattere. When they boarded a vaporetto, they were very careful to find seats inside. Leah tried to hide it as best as she could, but she was still a bit shaken by what happened on the way to Mrs Toffolo's. Her honorary aunt decided to have another

60

outing together the following day. If Leah ended up standing outside, she had overcome the shock of the accident; if she did not, they would talk about it.

Meanwhile, there was something else they had to discuss. They sat down; the countess loved the location. She sat facing the island of San Giorgio. The canal was bustling with traffic. Deborah Camerini enjoyed the view when she was a child and still enjoyed it. She waited until Leah had started on her ice cream to bring up the real reason they had a treat.

"Leah, do you have any plan for your future? What would you like to do?"

Leah looked at her ice cream as if it were an exciting piece of art. She was silent for a few minutes; then she looked up with a sombre expression on her face.

"My dream is perhaps too ambitious, and it will have to wait until my memory returns. My more realistic plan is to become a nurse. I was in the hospital for three months after the war with many other survivors from the camps, and remember the nurses very fondly; I thought they were our angels."

"They were, but what about the dream?"

"In the refugee camp, the one where Franco Cantoni found me, I started talking to a doctor who was helping me figure out what made me lose my memory. I would love to be a doctor who helps people who have gone through terrible things and have not stopped thinking about them."

"Why is it a dream?"

"I need to go to school for that. I do not remember how old I was or where I lived when I was deported. I know I must have lost many years of school, and I must go to school to make my dream come true."

The countess was overjoyed, and trying very hard to hide it. She wanted to bring up the subject of school or training with

Leah, but she did not expect the young woman to serve it to her on a silver platter.

"Would you like to go back to school?"

"I would love to study, but wouldn't know how to deal with questions from other people my age who did not go through my version of hell."

The countess realised why Leah had insisted on long sleeves for her summer dresses. More things were bothering Leah besides her lack of memory of anything that happened to her before the camps. But she had a solution. Truth be told, she had been planning the solution for a few days.

"We may organise tutors, so you could study without leaving home. Once you feel more relaxed with people your age and your tutors say you are ready, you will sit for an exam to attend a regular school."

"But what if I am not the Leah Mustaki you are looking for?"

"You are you, and I will organise tutors for you, Leah, or no Leah. If you are not Leah Mustaki, once you recover your memory, I may have a hard time changing how I call you, but I hope you will be patient and indulge me. Until you decide to leave, you are staying with me."

"How long does my visa last?"

"My legal cavalry will sort out the legal stuff when the time comes. Meanwhile, you could have a chat with Diana Mendes. She studied for over a year to go back to school with people her age. Racial laws and the war meant she would have been three years behind everybody else."

The countess sounded very determined to help Leah. Leah wondered aloud why she was so eager to help her. After all, if she turned out not to be Leah, they had known each other for less than a month. The countess stopped eating her ice cream, lifted her head, and started looking towards the island of San

Giorgio above Leah's head. Leah felt that the woman who had volunteered to be her honorary aunt and care for her was looking into her past. After what felt like a long silence, the countess lowered her head and looked at Leah. She smiled with a very warm facial expression, but her voice was very sombre.

"I made it. I hid in my home. Those who knew my real identity protected me. My children made it to Switzerland. After the war, those who helped me gave me all my assets back. I was lucky, and my family was lucky. "

The countess looked at what was left of her ice-cream as if it were a work of art. Leah was sure she was still looking into her past.

"Many others were not that lucky. Before I met you, I decided I owed it to them to help you. If you are Leah, you were twelve the last time I saw you. If you are not Leah, I met you about a month ago. Whoever you are, I like you, your choice of books, what you notice when we walk around, and your taste in art and music. I am more and more determined to help you. Do you mind?"

It was Leah's turn to be silent; the countess was getting worried. Leah ate the last spoonful of her ice cream, smiled at the countess, and spent a little longer with her thoughts before replying,

"I enjoy being in Venice, and am growing fond of living with you, Tonia, and the rest of your family. I have no idea who I am, or whether I shall ever remember my past. I feel safe with you; it gives me a feeling of family. No, I do not mind you helping me. I am very grateful. I hope one day to do something that will show my gratitude to you."

The countess decided it was time to go home; she had to do something; otherwise, she would have cried in public and ruined her face, something she could not allow to happen.

She summoned the waiter and paid; they both stood up and walked to the vaporetto stop to go home.

The following morning, the countess rang Rachele to find out whether the papers allowing Leah to stay in the country would need to be changed if she turned out not to be Leah Mustaki, after all. Rachele was in a hurry; she had to be in court. The case for the restitution of the assets seized from Emanuele Mendes and Gemma Mustaki was being heard that morning. Rachele suggested they discuss it the next time they had coffee.

Chapter Seven

July 1948

It was a very hot and humid day. A day you realise why, at the time of the Most Serene Republic, wealthy Venetians used to escape Venice in the summer for their villas in the countryside. The oppressive heat and the mosquitos were Palladium's greatest allies in getting work from those wealthy families who built beautiful summer residences within easy reach of Venice.

Gabriele and Rachele were taking the children to the beach. The countess thought it would have been a great way to get Leah and her cousins together and see what happened. On the vaporetto to the Lido, Leo and Mario were busy talking as usual. Paola and Diana invited Leah to sit with them and Mila. Davide was looking at photos of cars in a magazine. Rachele and the countess observed the interaction between Leah and the other children. All the Mendes children knew what the numbers tattooed on Leah's arm meant; they were unlikely to ask questions. There was not a hint of recognition between Paola and Leah. The countess remarked Paola looked like her maternal grandmother, hoping that Leah would remember how her paternal grandmother looked. She should not have been a disturbing memory.

Rachele had resumed her role as the legal advisor of the company that owned the Excelsior Hotel. They were at the beach in style. The countess was in her element, playing the grand old lady to perfection, sitting in the shade, reading a book. From time to time, she would summon Leo or Mario to fetch a waiter or get a drink for her at the bar. Deborah Camerini had invited everybody to lunch and asked the hotel to organise it on the beach rather than at the restaurant. The hotel obliged.

As the day progressed, it was also clear that there was no mutual recognition between Leah and her cousins Mario and Paola. Gabriele had vetoed an introduction explaining the story; Paola was still working with Doctor Corinaldi to stop her recurring nightmares and the guilt of surviving when her parents died. The doctor had advised against discussing her uncle, aunt, and cousin. On the way back, Leah joined Mario and Leo. They were all sixteen; there was no hint of recognition from Mario, who had adjusted to the idea of having survived when many others did not far better than his sister. When the countess and Leah got off the Vaporetto, Gabriele moved closer to Rachele, speaking in a low voice,

"I like Leah. After a while, she interacted with our lot very well. She was very good with Mila; but I do not think she is Leah Mustaki."

Years of practice of trying to have private conversation and supervise their children made Rachele move closer to her husband and whisper in an equally low voice.

"I like her as well; but if you are right, Joshua's father is the heir."

~

Zvi Treves and Alex Modiano were having a drink in a café in Cannaregio. They were sitting outside in the Fondamenta

Ormesini, along Canal de la Misericordia, away from the tourists' beaten paths. The day was getting less hot, and the evening promised to be pleasant. Zvi talked about Vienna divided into occupation zones and how different the atmosphere was when one left the part of town where the Russians were in charge. Alex reminded him that their grandparents were trying to reclaim their flat in the Russian occupation zone. They had their doubt they could keep it, but Alex's father (and Zvi's uncle) thought that recovering it had a substantial emotional and symbolic value for their grandparents. They were discussing their memory of the flat in Vienna when Alex noticed Joshua Schwartz cross the bridge from the Ghetto Novo. Zvi decided it was time he met the 'mysterious nephew,' so when Joshua turned towards them, Alex caught his attention and gestured to Joshua to join them for another drink. Zvi pulled a chair between him and Alex, and Joshua sat down. The conversation was relaxed, but Alex had the gut feeling that Zvi was trying to figure out Joshua Schwartz. They ordered another round of drinks, then Zvi mentioned he had met Joshua before.

"Your Schwarz grandfather and my Treves grandfather were friends; I remember seeing you when you were about two. It was the last time my grandfather took me to his favourite café in Trieste, the day before we made aliyah. You won't remember; you were barely talking."

"I vaguely remember my grandparents and the rest of my Italian family. My family left Italy when I was ten and we have never been back to visit. I am the first one to be back in Venice and I am sort of discovering vague childhood memories of my parents' tales of their lives in Italy."

Joshua kept fidgeting as he spoke; Alex could not help but notice he was not relaxed anymore. He kept looking at his watch. After what he thought was an acceptable time, he stood up.

"I have made plans to have dinner with two friends from the US Army who are travelling around Europe before being sent back to the States."

Alex looked at his watch

"It is almost dinnertime. We have to go as well."

They stood up and started walking towards Fiamma's home, talking about what they would have for dinner. They had just turned into Fondamenta del Ghetto when Zvi abruptly changed the subject.

"I have the gut feeling that Joshua could not wait to find an excuse to leave us."

At five am, Anita was getting ready to go to the fish market. In the summer, she enjoyed being out in the early morning hours before the heat and humidity became too much to bear. Her own personal breakfast was the lull before the storm. As usual, Anna had already left, leaving things in the oven for her. Anita was sipping her coffee and was surprised to see Diana up so early; she was in the middle of the end of high school exams[1]. Anita looked at her and realised she had not slept well. Coffee was still hot. She poured Diana a cup, gave her a slice of the cake that Anna had prepared an hour earlier, and sat in front of her. They sat in silence until Diana had finished her coffee. Anita realised how tense Diana was and was reluctant to leave her alone to go to the fish market. She started talking about what fish she hoped to find to distract Diana from the thought of whatever test she had to sit for that morning. Anita waited to leave for the fish market until Rachele and Gabriele appeared in the kitchen. They did not expect to see their daughter already up. Gabriele kissed Diana on the forehead and started sorting cups and saucers; Diana got up to help him. They talked about the test she would have that day; Philosophy was not her favourite subject. She was worried. Rachele was reassuring her when they heard the phone ring; Anita picked it up on her way out. She came back into the kitchen; it was Alvise Cantoni. Rachele picked up the kitchen extension. Alvise's voice sounded annoyed.

"When I arrived at the office, the front door was damaged. Somebody broke in during the night. The partners' offices are a mess; it doesn't look they had the time to look at the safe we have in our offices, but I cannot be sure."

Rachele tried to keep a matter-of-fact voice

"Either Gabriele or I will be there as soon as possible. Anita has gone to the market, Diana has one of her final exams today, we cannot both leave."

She put the phone down, turned to Gabriele

"Somebody broke into the office. I need to check my safe. If you are worried they might have interfered with any of your files, you can go and I wait for Anita to come back."

Diana stood up

"My exam is at 10. I shall not collapse in a heap of nerves if I am left alone for an hour. You can both go."

Rachele and the countess had settled for a café in Cannaregio for their regular chats. The countess had discovered this place between two canals behind the Ghetto. She loved the décor; it reminded her of the time before World War I, and Rachele loved they had a table in an inner courtyard so they could sit outside, in the shade, but away from passers-by. They both loved the quality of the cakes and not just because the café owner was a client of Anna, Rachele's daughter; they did not know that the first time they were there. As usual, the conversation was very mundane until the waiter brought their order. The countess had something she was eager to discuss with Rachele.

"Yesterday, we were on our way to Rialto market. It was early in the morning, and Leah wanted to walk there. She loves crossing the Rialto bridge; she finds it very familiar."

"I know where the Cantonis live; she would have crossed it each time she went to their home to play with Lisa."

"Anyway, we were crossing Rialto bridge when Leah fell over. This time, I am pretty sure somebody pushed her. I could not see the man very well; I can only tell you he was tall, with black hair, was not wearing a hat, was wearing a short-sleeved shirt, and he was rather muscular. He was running, but it could not have been an accident. He did not bump into her. I was talking to her and clearly saw his hand pushing her."

Rachele was sipping her coffee; she had to gain time and hide a smile (the countess had noticed that the man was 'pretty muscular')

"Poor girl, I now wonder if what happened on your way to Mrs Toffolo was also not an accident. Did you ever have the gut feeling somebody followed you?"

"I can't say I have, but who would follow us?"

"I do not know yet. Do you mind if I discuss it with the others?"

The countess said she would not, which allowed Rachele to mention what she wanted to talk about

"Mario and Paola did not recognise Leah, and Leah did not recognise them. There are a hundred plausible explanations for it, but would you be too distressed if she turned out not to be Leah Mustaki?"

Now it was Deborah Camerini's turn to gain time. She took a piece of the slice of strawberry cake she had in front of her. She took her time eating it, took a napkin to remove crumbs from her mouth, checked that she had not smudged her lipstick, and put the mirror away.

"I have seen her distress when she does not remember something she ought to. I have heard her nightmares, and I do not doubt her good faith. If she were pretending, she would be the greatest actress in history. As I said many times, she is a young survivor in distress, Leah, or no Leah. I am growing fond of her, whoever she is. Strangely enough, Sarah agrees with me, and we seldom agree on our assessment of people."

Rachele had to smile at the way the countess had brought up her daughter to reinforce her statement and hinted at her dislike of her daughter's husband at the same time. There was now a more important issue to discuss.

"Do we tell Joshua Schwartz that his father may be the heir?"

The countess took a sip from the glass of water that came with the coffee to buy time; she had finished the cake and the coffee.

"Can we wait? We do not know for sure Leah is not Leah Mustaki. Also, I was surprised that there was no hint of recognition when Joshua met me. Even if he does not remember me, I am sure his parents mentioned me. I have been in regular correspondence with them before and after the war; I have not seen him since he was twelve. His father sent my husband a photo of his bar mitzvah party, but even that was about ten years ago. As far as I can tell, he could be Joshua, but I am bothered that he did not recognise me."

Rachele's professional mind filed this information for later. She added it to her nephews' comments about what happened a few evenings earlier. She had not shared that information with her honorary aunt.

While waiting for the bill, they talked about Roberto's son. The conversation continued as they walked to the Sant'Alvise vaporetto stop. Rachele was returning to the office; the countess was picking up Leah from one of her tutors who lived nearby.

Gabriele and Rachele were first in the office, so Gabriele collected the mail. They were in Rachele's office sorting the mail together. She gave him the letters that concerned the firm's administration; he handed her the ones relating to clients' cases. They did not open letters addressed to Alvise, Roberto, Alex, or Franco. Gabriele passed on to Rachele a letter coming from the United States. Rachele opened it just when Alvise walked into the office. She dropped it on her desk and called out to her partner, urgency in her voice. When Alvise walked into her office, he wondered what had happened. Rachele said,

"Guido Schwartz wrote us a letter to tell us that his son had been demobbed and left for the United States before he received his original letter. He has now booked a passage back to Europe; he will leave on the 20th of July for Southampton and continue to Venice by train."

It took Alvise a few minutes to let the news sink in; he sat down, looked at Rachele first, then at Gabriele, and said,

"So, who is the young man we call Joshua Schwartz?"

When Roberto arrived, the three partners decided that discussing what to do with the young man impersonating Joshua Schwartz took priority over everything else. They asked the receptionist to rearrange or cancel their morning appointments and gathered in Rachele's office.

Alvise explained why they were there, and then Rachele took over.

"According to aunt Deborah, somebody is trying to harm Leah. There have been two accidents; our honorary aunt is not prone to drama; I am inclined to believe her. Also, she would have recognised the young man impersonating Joshua Schwartz."

Alex had been standing by the door; he moved to the table and sat down with his notepad and pen.

"What if he is not acting alone?"

Alex was about to say something when Franco interrupted him

"We do not know who broke into our office. Do you think somebody is watching us? Monitoring when we arrive or leave the office?"

Alvise was worried that his son and Rachele's nephew would get carried away.

"Nobody has broken any law yet. The young man has chosen his words carefully, and we have not shared with him anything that was not already publicly available if somebody knew where to look."

Alex took Alvise's words for what they were, reminding them to keep their feet firmly on the ground.

"Everybody in this room has been active in the resistance; we spent at least a couple of years wondering whether somebody was watching or following us. It should not be a problem to figure out if somebody is watching the office, or we are followed."

Gabriele looked at Rachele, who nodded.

"We are close friends or part of the same family; it would not look odd if you came to visit one evening. We could also ask my closest friend Paolo Mondani, who was also at school with Alvise and me, and his wife Sofia to help us. Paolo was in the resistance, too. Our young man, Joshua Schwartz's impersonator, never met them. You can all come to dinner in a couple of days."

Rachele added, smiling

"We need a couple of days. Otherwise, Anita will complain for weeks! Paolo and Sofia can help us check if somebody is watching the office. We also must inform aunt Deborah as soon as possible; she has to keep Leah safe without alarming her. The young man impersonating Joshua Schwartz never convinced her; she will tell us she was right several times."

Gabriele looked at his brother, smiling.

"Perhaps her golden boy and her favourite female lawyer could go. If I join you, she might think somebody died."

Rachele and Roberto looked at each other. Alvise lightened up the atmosphere; he looked at his friend and said,

"Chicken!"

Everybody was laughing when the receptionist knocked at the door to tell Alvise and Roberto she could not cancel their next meeting with a big corporate client.

Chapter Eight

July 1948

The previous evening, Rachele had to use all the experience she had gained managing witnesses in court and many children. She had decided that they had 90 minutes to discuss the 'fake Joshua Schwartz' and then have dinner with the family. Aunt Anita and Diana ensured that children and other guests were entertained during that time. Rachele got up early and walked to work alone. She needed time by herself to think everything through. Usually, she could see the wood and the trees, but she had to be confident about what was what. This time, however, she was not sure whether she had an overall picture as clear in her head as some of the details. If the 'wood' was unclear. How could she know whether she was missing any 'tree'?

She opened the door to the law firm with her keys; the empty office felt cooler than the outside world. She went to her office and sat down at her desk, started drawing circles, each one representing a detail. They represented the metaphorical trees. She was hoping they would help her see the shape of the metaphorical wood. After a while, there were several rings on the page, some connected to others, but she still could not see the wood. She had used the same logic most of her professional life, a technique to examine contracts she learnt fron one of her professors at University. She was so absorbed in her thoughts and her circles she had lost the sense of time. Alex startled her when he knocked at her door.

"Last night, I thought of something I wanted to discuss with you as soon as possible. I called your home and aunt Anita told me you had gone to the office very early. I made coffee for both of us."

Rachele looked at him as if she had just woken up.

"A Modiano never says no to a coffee. I am grateful for the interruption; I cannot figure out the overall picture; concentrating on something else might help."

 Alex put the empty coffee cups back on the tray, put the tray on a side table, and sat down opposite his aunt.

"Before you show me your circles, I have been thinking of something we discussed last night. Assuming that Leah's accidents were an attempt to get a rival heir out of the way, what if somebody helped the fake Joshua Schwartz? What if we are dealing with more than one person? "

Rachele was looking at her circles as she listened to him.

"Those are some of the questions I asked myself earlier."

Alex did not have notes, but his thoughts were very clear in his head.

"Then I remembered the first time Zvi bumped into him at the office. He looked at him as if he had met him before, but could not figure out who he was. I know Zvi met Joshua Schwartz when he was twelve and Joshua was two. Twenty-four years later, he could not think he recognised the young man from the toddler; he must have met him somewhere else. So, do we ask Zvi for help?"

Rachele lent back on the chair and joined her hands, her two index fingers touching her lips. It was a clear sign she was thinking. A few minutes later, she sat upright.

"I wonder if Zvi may even help us figure out how the fake Joshua Schwartz knew so much about the real one and how he could have that letter with the power of attorney."

Alex was smiling; he loved when he had answers to his aunt's questions. Most of the times, it worked the other way.

"I figured some of it out. Guido Schwartz told us that the real Joshua Schwartz never received his letter because he had already left his post; the fake Joshua Schwartz must have got hold of the letter somehow."

Rachele added something to her note before speaking

"Yes, but how? Also, did he get hold of the letter, or did somebody else? After all, we have somebody that could look like Joshua Schwartz. Most of us remember a boy with red hair and grey eyes. The man we met had red hair and grey eyes, and speaks Italian with an American accent...."

Alex started mocking an American accent.

 "Which could be imitated; remember, he never spent more than a couple of hours with us. Do we know where he is staying?"

"I think Alvise has his contact details here in Venice; what if we send Franco to have a look?"

"What if I go, claiming we need to talk to him? If he is in his room and I end up talking to him, I can always ask him for his availability for an update."

"If he is not there, try to find out whether he is staying with friends. Pretend you want to invite him to dinner. See if you can talk to Zvi this morning, share our conversations with him, and ask for his help. You can go together to the place where the fake Joshua Schwartz is staying."

Alex stood up; before he left the office, Rachele, the aunt replaced Rachele, the boss,.

"Take the coffee cups back to the kitchen, please, and be careful!"

~

When Alex and Rachele were having their conversation, Franco Cantoni was on his way to have breakfast with the countess and Leah. The previous evening, they had decided that somebody would have to follow Leah to make sure she was safe; Franco volunteered while they were looking for private detectives. That morning, Leah had an hour with a tutor who did not live far away. She was used to walking on her own; it was close enough, familiar enough, and she knew her way.

That morning, they had to check if somebody was watching, so the countess walked with her, with Franco following at a distance. The two women had just turned into the Strada Nuova, a wide street that was a canal a few centuries earlier and had been filled in; Franco turned the corner a couple of minutes after them. Following the countess's large straw hat and her unmissable yellow blouse with green leaves. He noticed a man looking at magazines by the newsagents, who started walking when the two ladies walked past him. Franco was pretty sure he could remember his face. The man wore a white shirt with blue trousers like many other passers-by; when Franco started following him, he noticed a bald patch on the back of his head that a recent haircut did not hide. He focused on it.

Just as the ladies were crossing the bridge over Rio San Felice, the man started walking faster. He climbed the steps two by two, reached the countess and Leah, stretched his left arm, and pushed Leah before running away. The countess was ready and held on to Leah, keeping her steady; the bridge balustrade did the rest. Leah grabbed it, stopping her from falling down the steps into Campo San Felice. Franco had started running when he noticed the man walking faster, but was not fast enough to see where the man had gone. He retraced his step to see if the countess and Leah were fine. The three of them went into a nearby café where they could recover; Leah was shaken, but fine. Ten minutes later, they continued the walk to Leah's tutor, the young woman walking between Franco and the countess. Franco volunteered to come back by the end of Leah's lesson; he had books with him and would study in a nearby café.

Three men were having a drink in a bar on the eastern side of Giudecca Island, near a boatyard. They had chosen that place because they had a very low chance of being seen by anybody from the law firm or somebody else who had met Joshua Schwartz. Besides its location, it was a worker's cafe, a place where the countess was not likely to set foot, or so they thought. They were not paying much attention to their voices; they were not speaking Italian. Anton, the oldest of the three, was annoyed at one of the other two.

"Herbert, you said they were ready for you. How come? You told me that the previous accident you provoked at Rialto bridge was unsuccessful because a passer-by caught her before she hit the pavement."

Herbert, the man wearing a white shirt and blue trousers, tried to say something and then stopped. Anton continued his tirade and then turned to Bruno, the red-haired one of the group.

"We need to change our tactic; you say it will be long before assets can be sold and you can cash the inheritance. Did they give you any idea of how long it should take?"

Bruno had been silent for a while; he was nervous.

"They are talking months before all the court cases have been heard, then we need to wait until sales go through. Also, it does not matter; if the daughter is alive, she will inherit everything."

Anton looked annoyed.

"I understand the daughter may not be the daughter. She lost her memory and may not be Leah Mustaki after all. Do not lose your nerve and continue pretending to be Joshua Schwartz. We just must bide time, and we have the resources to wait."

That seemed to bring the conversation to an end. Anton, the leader of the group, asked for the bill in Italian and added an insult in his language, watching if the barman reacted in any way. He wanted to make sure the man behind the counter could not understand them, but could not know that the police were watching the boatyard looking for smugglers. The barman was a police informer; he had understood everything they said, including the insult he had taken for the test it was. He did not think they had done anything of concern to the police, or at least not yet. If they returned, he would make a point of listening to what they were saying. In the meantime, he tried to memorise as much as he could of the three men. He wanted to be sure he could recognise them if they came back.

It was the end of the business day. Roberto, Franco, and Alex were in Rachele's office to discuss the day's events. Roberto had very little to contribute; they had filed petitions to each relevant court for all the assets listed in the wills. They had petitioned as the estate. Now it was just a matter of waiting until the cases were heard in court; they had time to figure out who the heir was. Franco related what happened to Leah that morning. He was reasonably confident that nobody had followed them on their way home and wondered whether the countess or the estate would fund somebody to protect Leah. He thought they needed a professional.

Rachele had listened to Franco Cantoni. Her hands joined, her two index fingers touching her lips. She pulled herself upright, took out the chart with all the circles, and wrote something. She then looked first at Franco, then at Alex.

"So far, we know that somebody is trying to harm Leah. We do not know if it is associated with the fake Joshua Schwartz or somebody else, maybe tied to Leah's other identity. Alex, did you find any evidence that our mystery man is working with somebody else?"

Alex had been to the address that the fake Joshua Schwartz had given to the law firm. It was a room rented near the freight yard, close to Piazzale Roma, the furthest truck drivers or freight trains could get in the old city, near where vehicles could take the ferry to the Lido. It was one of the nearest places to the bridge to the mainland. Alex had wandered in saying he had a message for Joshua Schwartz, the date and time of a meeting at the law firm. Zvi was standing outside, keeping the reception desk in full view, just in case Alex needed help. The receptionist was not very talkative; when Alex suggested Mr Schwartz's friend could also receive the message, the receptionist told him he was the only one who had come looking for Mr Schwartz during the time he had been staying with them.

Rachele had been taking notes. She stood up, walked around her desk, and lent on it.

"It is unusual for a visitor to stay in that area; it is almost as if he needs to travel to and from the mainland at no notice. I wonder if he has a car or if he regularly meets somebody who drives from the mainland and does not want to leave the car in one of the covered parking spaces."

Alex had something else to add to his report.

"On our way back home for lunch, Zvi wondered if we needed some help. He was sure one of his contacts could organise somebody to watch the fake Joshua Schwartz's lodging and offered to find out how much that would cost us."

Roberto and Franco noticed Rachele had not reacted to Alex mentioning Zvi Treves's contacts. Almost as if they expected him to have some in Venice, Rachele saw their expression and nodded to Alex, who continued.

"Aunt Rachele, Uncle Gabriele, and I have wondered whether there was more to Zvi's stay in Venice and his frequent trips to Vienna and Prague than his alleged plan to secure second-hand coffee roasting equipment."

Roberto Mendes was silent for a few minutes before making a comment

"You did not think to ask him. You think that the Italian authorities may not like whatever he is up to."

Rachele looked like the cat who ate the canary.

"We do not know what he is up to, and we decided it was in our interest to keep it that way. Alex, just let us know how much his contacts ask."

"Can't we go to the police?"

"I do not think we have enough facts to go to the police. Maybe Vice-Commissario De Antoni would listen to me just to be polite, but at the moment, we have no actual evidence.

Just Franco, who saw a man push Leah as she and Aunt Deborah crossed a bridge."

Franco stood up to close the shutters. It might be late afternoon, but the sun was still hot. On his way back to the table, he asked what Alex and Roberto wanted to ask.

"Why don't we have enough? What have we established so far?"

Rachele looked at him, sighed and tried her best not to sound patronising to somebody whom she had known since he was born.

"What we have now is clear on the surface. We have somebody pretending to be Joshua Schwartz; obviously, he wants to lay his hands on the inheritance. There is nothing to inherit until we have recovered all the assets. Things may change in a few months. Maybe a man has been trying to hurt the young woman we know as Leah Mustaki three times. We do not know who that man is or what his motives are and still have no evidence that leads us to believe that the two are connected."

She looked at her notes.

"We also do not know how they know so much about the estate and the heirs. I hope that by the time we summon our friendly police detective, we have something more substantial than our thoughts."

She closed her notepad. A sign that the meeting was over. Roberto looked at the time and realised he had to go home. Alex invited Franco to have a drink with him and Zvi. Gabriele chose that moment to appear at the door, asking his wife if she was ready to go home. When they walked out of the building, they all checked the Riva to see if there was a man who looked like the person Franco had described to them earlier.

Chapter Nine

July-August 1948

Rachele was sitting in what had become her favourite café in Venice. The courtyard with the two trees provided an opportunity to be outside in the shade with some privacy, something unusual in Venice. She had been waiting for the countess for ten minutes; Deborah Camerini was rarely late. Rachele started wondering whether something had happened when her honorary aunt appeared in the courtyard, followed by the waiter. She could not help but smile at the sight of the countess talking to her 'favourite waiter', who was rather good-looking, probably in his early twenties. As usual, they started talking about family. Aunt Deborah was looking for something in her handbag. She took out a business card and showed it to Rachele.

"I was thinking of giving Diana something from this shop as a gift for a successful end to her high school exams."

Rachele knew better than trying to stop her.

"Please wait, Diana still does not know how she did in her exams."

The waiter arrived with a slice of the 'cake of the day', their coffees, and two glasses of water; after he went back inside, they felt free to talk.

"Did anything happen? You are seldom late."

"I am not used to having a guardian angel. I did not realise how much it would slow me down."

Rachele thought that her honorary aunt was making even more of an effort to look perfect because of the guardian angels, i.e., the young men hired as bodyguards for her and Leah. After they had the first sip of coffee, Rachele started relating what they had discussed the previous evening at work. The countess was intrigued, but did not look concerned.

"I know that the estate has a considerable value, but I did not expect a plot to get hold of it. Who do you think is behind it?"

Rachele expected that question; she was ready.

"At the moment, we are not even sure that the man who has pushed Leah at least twice and the fake Joshua Schwartz work together. If they do, they have underestimated the time to turn those assets into cash."

"Why would they want to sell?"

"Selling assets must be part of the strategy of any heir; they must fund the taxes, and I am sure they plan to keep selling. They have at least a six months wait before they can start turning anything into cash. The court is likely to prioritise the assets of the living or heirs that want to continue using it."

"Why would they not prioritise us?"

"A sixteen-year-old daughter, who will need a guardian until she turns 21, or a brother who lives in the United States, can hardly justify a priority hearing, and there are many people in the queue."

The countess took out a small notepad, pulled out the pencil attached to it, and looked for a blank page.

"Do you have an idea how long we have to wait before the court discusses Raffaele's and Sylvia's assets?"

Rachele took out her diary from her handbag.

"Emanuele and Gemma had a less complex estate. The hearing to recover their assets on behalf of Mario and Paola is in early October, almost two years after we petitioned on their behalf. Myriam got her home back in less than two months."

"So, time is on our side?"

Rachele took a folder from her attaché case, opened it, and checked the dates.

"We started filing petitions in January. The first court cases are coming up in October, but they are the safe and less valuable assets. We had to be a hundred percent sure that the most valuable assets were still in their unencumbered possession when they were seized, so we filed our petitions last March. The court scheduled the hearing for February next year. Bear in mind that in all cases, we stated you were funding all the costs, and, for your sake, we had to have as fast a resolution as possible."

"But I am lucky enough to be able to afford it."

Rachele smiled in a conspiratorial way, lowered her voice, and said, only half-joking.

"Does the Revenue know about all your profits as an art dealer? You can tell me; I am your lawyer, and our conversations are privileged."

The countess lowered her voice; her face and tone were indignant; her smile was telling otherwise.

"What do you think? It is official if I sell or buy through an auction house, but private sales are a different matter altogether. Anyway, the real Joshua Schwartz called me last night from Southampton."

Rachele almost dropped her cup of coffee.

"How do you know he is the real Joshua Schwartz?"

The countess smiled

"He called me 'Aunt Deborah' and used the Italian version of his name; I knew they changed his name from Giosuè to Joshua because the Italian version of that name is almost impossible to pronounce in English. The fake Joshua Schwartz kept claiming he had no memory of his time in Venice. The person who called me last night asked me if he could stay with me, and he is looking forward to meeting Leah. The fake Joshua Schwartz declined my offer of hospitality. He might have been concerned I would catch him out, and he needs his freedom to meet people with no scrutiny."

"So, did he tell you when he joins us in Venice?"

"I am afraid I told him to spend a few days in London and then let you know. He will call the law firm after he confirms his travel plans."

Rachele joined her hands, index fingers touching her lips. The countess was well aware she was thinking, so she waited for her comment. Rachele took her time sipping some water before speaking.

"We need to make sure he does not meet the fake Joshua Schwartz for a while, not until we have found out more about what they are planning, whoever they are. We also need to protect him, and may have to come to you to meet him the first time rather than have him come to the office. If they think Leah is a threat, they may ensure he has some accidents. We need to make sure he stays safe."

Rachele wanted her honorary aunt to understand how serious she was about the need to protect Leah and the real Joshua; she continued after a brief pause.

"I wonder if Alex, Franco, or anybody else can find out what name the fake Joshua Schwartz used to book his accommodations. We need to stop calling him 'the fake Joshua Schwartz.' It is too much of a mouthful."

The countess was drinking water; she stopped.

"What if we call him Mister X?"

"We already have a Mister X, the man with the bold patch who pushed Leah."

"Can we call him the Unnamed?"

"Like the character from *The Betrothed*[1]?"

The countess was now checking her makeup. Rachele did not see her guardian angel, but she suspected he was a young man. After putting her mirror away, the countess had the last word, as usual.

"Except we are not afraid of him; we are just careful. He should be afraid of us."

Rachele had returned to the office. The day was hot and humid as a sunny July day in Venice can be. She was having a drink in the kitchen, thinking of which route home had the longest stretches in the shade; she was not looking forward to her and Gabriele walking home in the glaring sunlight. Suddenly, the front door to the office slammed open; Rachele heard Diana's excited voice asking the receptionist where her parents were. Gabriele heard it too. They both appeared in the corridor before the receptionist could answer. Diana looked at them, a massive grin on her face.

"I passed with an average of eight and a half out of ten. Angelo Baldan thinks I am in the top five of our class, but I was too relieved and excited, and only looked at my results."

Gabriele and Rachele hugged their daughter, and the rest of the office applauded; Diana took a bow. Her parents had a meeting, so Gabriele suggested she use his office to call Aunt Anita; later, they would all walk home to lunch.

At the end of the month, Gabriele updated the partners on the financial aspect of all their cases. The conversation was about billing, expenses, and what they could claim back from their clients. Gabriele and Rachele lingered a bit after the meeting; they were not serious when they told Diana off for calling her sister Emma in South America with the news, then the three of them made their way home, large hats and sunglasses their only defence from the glaring sunshine.

The three men were back in the café by the boatyard. They were the only customers at that time of the day. It was too late for post-lunch coffee and too early for pre-dinner (or after-work) drinks. They had arrived one by one, sitting inside to escape the afternoon heat thanks to the three large ceiling fans. They were away from the tourist part of Venice and likely to be the only foreigners there, so they could speak freely and without whispering. This time, the conversation was not just about the Schwartz estate; they were talking about a consignment that was supposed to arrive at the commercial harbour in Marghera, waiting for shipment to Spain. The barman was cleaning the counter but was not missing a word of what they were saying. The conversation was getting animated; the older one of the three turned to the red-headed one.

"Bruno, you must admit, it was difficult to smuggle the consignment into Italy this time. We had to have convincing and realistic false paperwork, which is why everything is two days late."

The third man intervened.

"Anton, the ship sails in two days. If the consignment does not arrive today, it may be difficult to smuggle it on board."

The barman thought Bruno was not the group leader; maybe he was the brain.

"Herbert, we have changed the suppliers of paperwork. We now work with people in Vienna. I understand the delay. Anton, this is very risky. You know, it is more difficult to smuggle people on board in the last two days before the ship sails."

"But, Bruno, they are not clandestine. We have paid for their passage."

"Yes, but the Italian authorities do not know who is sailing to Spain on board a cargo ship, and we do not know how much luggage they are taking with them. Speaking of risk, I think they have figured out we are after the young woman. This morning, I noticed somebody following them during their trip to the market, and it was not Herbert. We need to be cleverer if we want to get rid of my fake cousin."

The man known as Anton laughed out loud.

"Yes, Bruno, the fake Joshua Schwartz is trying to get rid of the fake Leah Mustaki."

The barman recognised them; this time he had information the police could use. He tried memorising the three men's faces as much as he could. He also noticed that Herbert had a bald patch on the back of his head and was by far the more muscular of the three. It was clear to him that somebody was pretending to be Joshua Schwartz; why? Who was Joshua Schwartz? He waited for the three men to leave the bar and called Vice-Commissario De Antoni.

Umberto de Antoni put the phone down. The name Leah Mustaki sounded familiar. He was sure he had not come across it in any of his cases, but had heard it before. His informer had heard people talking about smuggling, but was not sure whether they were smuggling goods out of Italy or people. He was concentrating on what the information he received might mean, then started drawing a circle and figured out why the name Leah Mustaki was so familiar. He picked up the phone and called Rachele Modiano, the woman he met as Rina von Moden in 1944, when they were both active in the resistance. After a brief conversation, Rachele suggested they meet at her office as soon as possible. It was mid-afternoon, Umberto realised that the law firm was on his way to Piazzale Roma to catch a bus to his home in Mestre, on the mainland. He left, telling his assistant where he was going, adding that he would go home from there.

Umberto took the vaporetto to Riva De Biasio. He had been living in Venice for only two years, but was still in awe each time he had to walk around town and still cherished the opportunity to sit outside in one of the front seats. He did not care if they mistook him for a tourist. His wife had talked him into moving away from the old city, but at least his office was still here. Being a police officer in Venice allowed him to experience the beauty of the place every day. The tannoy announcing his stop shook him from his reverie. He got off the vaporetto, crossed the Riva, and walked into the building. He liked Rachele and her husband and was looking forward to their conversation. He knocked on Gabriele's office to say hello; Rachele heard him and came out of hers to greet him. She then called Alex and Franco because they could provide some first-hand information. Umberto noticed Rachele took out a notepad with her circles; he knew it was a sign she had paused the social side till they had finished discussing the professional side of his visit. Umberto related his conversation with his informer, took out his notebook, and read the description of the three men. He realised the other three people in the room did not know who Anton was, but they had recognised the description of Bruno and Herbert provided by Umberto's informer. Rachele went out looking for her brother-in-law. Roberto came into the office, heard the description of Bruno, and agreed that it could be the person they had been referring to as the fake Joshua Schwartz, then left the room.

Rachele shared what they knew, prompting Alex and Franco to correct or expand some of her points if they thought it was relevant. Umberto took notes. Alex and Franco were smiling. Alex pointed to his aunt; Rachele was lying back on her chair; her hands joined, index fingers touched her lips, and her eyes closed; she was thinking. After a few minutes of comfortable silence in the room, she opened her eyes, straightened up, and drew a bigger circle on a separate piece of paper.

"We do not have many certainties, but, after a few assumptions, I think I can have an idea of a big picture; whether it is the correct big picture remains to be seen. Bruno and his teammates are involved in a movement that smuggles people out of Europe using Venice and maybe other ports in the Adriatic. We do not know who they are smuggling out and why they need to be smuggled out. I thought the surviving Nazis had already left Europe, but it may not be connected to that. They need money for their operation, and the Schwartz estate has the potential to give them a lot of cash."

Umberto was taking notes. Rachele paused to allow him to catch up.

"Leah is in the way, which is why they need to get rid of her. There is something that does not quite convince me, though. Umberto, you said that one of them mentioned the fake cousin, so they must know there are doubts about Leah's identity. Wouldn't it be easier to discredit her than kill her? Mind you, if they want to get rid of her, they are not doing a very good job, and I am very grateful for that."

Umberto nodded. He closed his notepad, put it in his briefcase, and stood up.

"Unfortunately, what I heard from my informer and from you does not warrant immediate police action."

Rachele smiled

"If Bruno were my client and got arrested, I would raise hell because the police acted on very weak circumstantial evidence."

It was now Umberto's turn to summarise; he nodded at Rachele, who nodded back. He smiled back.

"We have had two, maybe three, vague attempts to hurt Leah. I could describe each one of them as an accident. You now have somebody following Leah and the countess to protect them. We have a possible smuggling operation, and we only know that they will use a ship sailing for Spain in about two days."

Alex felt the need to intervene.

"We also have people that know a lot about the Schwartz family, but we do not know how they acquired their information."

Umberto nodded and closed his notepad.

"Our assumptions are enough to keep me intrigued and you careful and protective. In the meantime, I will see what I can find out about ships sailing for Spain in the next few days. I also see if I can check the record of the place where Bruno, otherwise known as the fake Joshua Schwartz, is staying."

Rachele added

"Needless to say, we now have to stay in touch."

Alex smiled and thought his aunt was now trying to have the last word; she was spending too much time with the countess. Umberto's comment surprised him.

"Of course, the quality of your refreshment is too good. Why don't I come back in a week? If there is any major development before then, one of us will call the other, and we can organise a meeting if necessary."

After Umberto left, Rachele asked Alex and Franco to stay. She wanted to discuss what they had just found out.

"Now we know it is likely that the name of the fake Joshua Schwartz is Bruno; we need to find out his surname. He does not work alone. We do not know yet how come he knows so much about the real Joshua Schwartz that he can impersonate him with some credibility, and how come they know that Leah Mustaki may not be Leah Mustaki after all."

Alex was drawing his circles on a notepad; Franco was the first to react.

"There are only four possible sources of the information that Leah Mustaki may not be Leah Mustaki. The Agency in Geneva, the Rabbi and his wife in the Displaced People camp, us, and the Pesaro De Bonfili household."

"Are you saying that the countess may be involved?"

"No, one of her staff may have overheard a conversation and discussed it with somebody else outside the household."

Alex stopped drawing.

"Aunt Rachele, are you sure you are the only one who knows the other identity of Leah? Franco and I know that the number tattooed on her arm had another name associated with it in the Nazi registers, but nobody shared with us what that name was."

"When Rav Lazar and his wife arrived in Venice with Leah, he paid me ten US Dollars to be the young woman's legal representative. Then he gave me her complete file, which had the other name and associated information. I decided not to share it with Aunt Deborah until I discussed it with the doctor who helped Paola; then, when the countess and I went to see Doctor Corinaldi, she told us to wait in case her memory improved. So, I kept it to myself, and the countess agreed. The file is in my locked cabinet; I am pretty sure nobody has looked at it."

"Do you still use hair to check that nobody else opened it?"

"Yes, but I'll never tell you where I put it and what I used to keep it in place."

Rachele stood up, the meeting over. She left her office, knocked at the doorpost of her husband's, and suggested that if he could stop for the day, they could go for a drink at the Zattere before going home for dinner.

It had been a sweltering day; the countess and Leah were on their way to dinner at Fiamma's. Leah enjoyed being around people. The Pesaro de Bonfili children and the Mendes clan gave her a sense of belonging to a family she did not remember, but the war took away. They had decided to walk; at that time of the evening, the vaporetto would have been very crowded, and being on the water would have made the humidity unbearable. They felt the heat under their feet and the humidity around them, even if it was past six o'clock in the evening. They were both aware of their minder behind them; the countess said that she hoped that Roberto Mendes had the sense to invite him to dinner. When they came out of

Calle del Pintor and were about to turn into Rio Terà Farsetti, they noticed that a lady walking ahead of them started staggering. She was walking alone. The countess sensed Leah was getting anxious and could not understand why. Suddenly the lady fainted, a heat stroke; somebody ran out of the nearby pharmacy to assist her.

Leah stopped walking, was breathing heavily, and was about to cry. She held on to the countess as if she were her life raft. The countess turned to their 'guardian angel,' who had noticed Leah's distress. He ran forward to help. When he came closer to them, Leah hung on to the countess even tighter, which alarmed Deborah Camerini. She started talking in a very soothing voice; she kept saying that the man was their friend; he was more than that; he was their guardian angel, and Leah should not be afraid. Leah kept staring at the woman who fainted.

Meanwhile, whoever was helping had revived her and was helping her back on her feet. Once she was standing, two passers-by helped walk her into the pharmacy. Leah was staring at the scene, breathing heavily, when the woman disappeared into the pharmacy. She spoke, her eyes wide open, staring at nothing.

"When they made us march with very little food and water, many people fainted; we were trying to revive them, but most of them were dead, and we had to leave them there. I fainted, but they revived me; later, when we were in the other camp, I saw different soldiers. I fainted again, woke up in the hospital, and did not remember anything. When a nurse came by, she called me Leah. I hope it is my name; you all love Leah."

The countess did not hesitate, not even for a second.

"We love you. It is irrelevant if your name is Leah, Rebecca, or Hermintrude. We love you, whatever your name is. Never forget that."

Before releasing her grip on Leah, she turned to the minder and mouthed, "Be ready to catch her."

She released her grip on the young woman. Her smile and the smile of their bodyguard were a sign that they were both relieved that Leah was still standing.

Chapter Ten

August 1948

Umberto de Antoni was out having coffee with a colleague who had just come back from two weeks in the Dolomites. The colleague was saying it was a great respite from the oppressive heat of Venice in the summer. Umberto missed a break in a cooler climate, but his wife was due in September, and they thought they had better stay home. His wife was now at a nearby beach with friends, and he was working. It was such a hot and humid morning that even the ceiling fans in the cafe were not providing any respite. Umberto thought of his wife at the beach with some envy. Suddenly, he stopped talking; he had seen a man who looked like the description of Bruno, the fake Joshua Schwartz. By now, four people had described him. Umberto merged all the descriptions in his head, and based on the features everybody agreed upon, he thought he was looking at Bruno. Except, the man was now speaking Italian with a slight German accent. He asked the barman how to go to La Fenice theatre. Bruno kept asking for clarification, something not uncommon for a tourist who had ended up near the Questura, not on the most beaten tourist routes, but not very far from them. Umberto's colleague noticed that his attention was now somewhere else; Umberto whispered to him he might have had an unexpected break in a case he was following. He explained he would try to see where that redhead was going. He hoped to be back in the office by lunchtime.

Luckily for Umberto, Bruno wore a burgundy shirt, an unusual colour worn by men in this heat. He was not wearing a hat, so the combination of red hair and burgundy shirt meant the policeman could not miss him in a crowd. Umberto followed him to a Campo near the Opera House. Bruno walked into a music shop; there was a café nearby where Umberto could sit in the shade and watch the shop. He showed his identification to the waiter, asked for a coffee and the bill, and sat there waiting, watching the shop, and enjoying the shade. Over an hour later, he saw Bruno leave. Thanks to Rachele and her team, Umberto knew where he lived, so he decided to find out what Bruno was doing in the shop. He walked in and showed his identification to the middle-aged woman he found behind the counter. Umberto knew many people had compared him to a young Gary Cooper. Although he was a one woman man, he had no problem flirting if that meant he could get more information from a woman. So, he smiled at the lady in the most seductive way he knew.

"I may have followed the wrong man most morning; who was the young man who spent so much time in this shop?"

The woman smiled back and adjusted her hair before talking. Umberto's smile became wider. The good-looking helpless policeman act was working once again,

"He is a student at the University. His name is Joseph Heber, from Switzerland, but his mother was born in Yugoslavia. His grandfather was a violinist in an orchestra in Maribor; he taught him to play when he was a child during his school holidays."

Umberto kept up the flirting helpless policeman act, hoping to get more information. It worked.

"He does not own a violin; he has no money to buy one, so once a week, he comes here and plays a violin we have for sale. He has been coming for the past three months; I love to hear him play; he is very good. Some people make a point of coming to the shop on Monday mornings when he comes to play."

Umberto would go back to the café and write what he remembered of the conversation in the small notepad he always carried with him. Meanwhile, he had to continue playing the good-looking, helpless policeman.

"Not the person I was supposed to follow; my boss will be mad at me. I love the violin; what does he play?"

"Most of the times, he plays Mozart pieces, sometimes by heart; sometimes I let him use one of the scores I sell. This morning, for instance, he played the first movement of 'A little night music'. It was perfect; I got lost in the music..."

Her face changed to a dreamy expression.

"… and I get lost in those grey eyes of his. I swim in those eyes, just as I am swimming in yours now."

Umberto thanked her, kissed her hand, and said he would be back on Monday because he loved the violin, and would love to listen to Joseph Heber. He walked out and decided against sitting at the same café because people in the shop could see him. He crossed a bridge, found himself near the staff entrance to La Fenice Theatre, Venice Opera House, walked inside, showed his identification, and asked the doorman if he could make a discrete phone call to his office. The doorman took him to a nearby empty office, saying that the person who works there was somewhere in the Alps and therefore, nobody would disturb him. Umberto sat at the desk and dialled his number; his assistant answered the phone.

"Bellini, can you please start checking if the University, the Conservatory or any other school in Venice has a Joseph Heber from Switzerland as a student? That is the name given by somebody who looked like the description of Bruno. We must establish if he is the man we know as Bruno or somebody else. We know Bruno sometimes uses another name."

His assistant had a message for him.

"A Franco Cantoni called, leaving an important message. He thinks he saw a man that could be Anton staring at the office from the other side of the Grand Canal. He saw it from the vaporetto for three days running. The man sits with an easel at the Fondamenta at the end of Calle dello Spezier. Not unusual in Venice except Franco wonders why somebody would like to paint buildings from the 1930s with no particular architectural value."

Umberto thanked him and said he would be back by lunchtime. He hung up and walked out, thanked the doorman who stopped him.

"I did not mean to eavesdrop on your conversation, but the name Joseph Heber got my attention. Three months ago, somebody with that name came and asked me if there were spare instruments for the orchestra, he lost his violin during the war in an air raid in Austria, and now he did not have the money to get one with his student budget. I pointed him to a music shop nearby."

"Are you sure of the name?"

"Yes, I am. The name the young man gave me was very similar to the name of a Swiss conductor, Joseph Hubert, who was going to be a guest conductor a month later."

"Thank you. Do you remember him well enough to describe him?"

"Sorry, I don't. I only saw him once for a few minutes. I just remembered him when I heard you say his name."

Umberto was now more determined than ever to go to the address they had for Joseph Heber/Bruno/Joshua Schwartz to see if he could find out which documents he used to check-in. He also was pretty sure that Joseph Heber was another false name. There was also the problem of the painter that had been painting one of the few scenes with nondescript buildings you could find in Venice. Was he Anton?

At his time of the year, Anita loved to go out as early as possible to buy bread and do her general shopping. Going to the baker near the synagogue for bread and then being one of the early customers at the Rialto market was pleasant at six o'clock in the morning when heat and humidity felt manageable, except that morning, they were not manageable even at six o'clock. She discussed it with the rest of the Mendes family as they drifted into the kitchen for breakfast. Mila, Paola, and Davide were the only ones sitting down, and Rachele was making sure they were drinking their milk and barley and not just eating the sponge cake Anna had made the previous evening. She was not paying attention to the conversation between Anita and Diana. When Gabriele walked in with the paper, she looked up just when Diana was making a comment about Sofia Mondani, one of her honorary aunts, one of Rachele and Gabriele's closest friends, the wife of Paolo Mondani, Gabriele's closest friend since childhood and the closest thing he had to another brother.

Rachele looked at Gabriele and said,

"Sofia could be the solution."

Gabriele, Diana, and Anita looked at each other. They could not figure out what Rachele meant. Gabriele was the first one to react.

"Do you care to share the beginning of your train of thoughts that ended with 'Sofia could be the solution,' or do we have to guess?"

Gabriele's comment made the five-year-old Mila giggle; Paola and Davide looked at her with the superiority of their twelve years. Rachele said that they would discuss it on their way to work. Gabriele reminded Diana that she should be at the office by nine; she was replacing the receptionist who was somewhere in the Alps. When Davide asked why they were not in the Alps, Anita explained that their uncle Michele Bolaffi was not feeling very well, and they had decided to stay in Venice just in case their aunt Myriam needed help. They were waiting for Mario and Leo to wake up, and then they would go to the beach with their cousins Enrico and Gloria Bolaffi. She was preparing their packed lunch while she was talking to them.

Gabriele and Rachele were ready to leave; Leo and Mario appeared half asleep, still in their pyjamas, as if summoned by Anita, just in time to receive a kiss on the forehead from Rachele and Gabriele. The two sixteen-year-olds cringed because they both thought they were past that. After kissing all the other children on the forehead, telling Diana they would see her later, and wishing Anita good luck taking seven youngsters to the beach, they were off.

It was not eight o'clock yet, but the heat and humidity hit them once they were out on the Campo; they took a longer route, more sheltered from the sun, hoping for some respite from the heat. They talked about how Anita was still at the centre of the well-oiled machine that was their family. Rachele then mentioned that Paolo and Sofia had been very kind to take Mila with them when they spent two weeks in the country as guests of the Contarinis. Mila somehow referred to Count and Countess Contarini as her 'grandparents in the countryside,' confusing everybody who was not part of their clan about how she could have three sets of grandparents. Mila had become a good friend of Alice Contarini, one of the Contarini's grandchildren, who was also five.

Speaking of Paolo and Sofia and the family who hosted them when they were hiding during the last two years of the war brought Gabriele back to Rachele's earlier statement that 'Sofia could be the solution.'

"Now that it is just the two of us care to share with me what problem Sofia will help you solve, and why?"

They had now turned into Calle Corner; Rachele took off her sunglasses, stopped walking, and moved her straw hat backwards to look at her husband.

"Sofia can chat up a piece of granite and get its life story in less than ten seconds. We have been wondering why somebody would want to paint the building where our office is with all the interesting buildings around Venice. Maybe Sofia would agree to take a walk to the end of Calle Dello Spezier and chat up the man who has been standing there with an easel for the past three days."

"The one Franco thinks is Anton, a teammate of the fake Joshua Schwartz?"

"The very one. I thought that if we invite Paolo and Sofia for drinks this evening, I can explain the situation and see if Sofia would like to help."

"You know she would, but I wonder if she has to do it alone."

"I doubt somebody is watching our home; Anita would have noticed. Sofia is safe. She has not come to the office in the past few months, and they have no way of linking her to us, but I'll let Umberto know just in case and make sure somebody is watching from our office. She must talk to him long enough to describe him to Umberto. We'll make sure she is safe."

Roberto had suggested they meet at his home, so they arrived one by one at Fondamenta del Ghetto in the mid-afternoon. Fiamma insisted they cool down in the sitting room before having a cold drink. Rachele, Gabriele, Paolo and Sofia Mondani, Alex, Franco, Alvise, Rachele, and Umberto de Antoni were all enjoying the less warm air of the sitting room, thanks to the two ceiling fans and four other table fans. Dina, Roberto's wife, made a brief appearance with cold drinks from a recipe from Fiamma's mother, lemon juice, fresh mint leaves, and cold water, then disappeared.

Umberto was there as a family friend, not as a policeman. He read the description of Anton; Paolo and Sofia Mondani agreed it was close enough to the man sitting with an easel in the same spot for the past four days. They said he had what looked like a watercolour of Ponte Degli Scalzi, but he maintained he sat there trying to sketch a vaporetto. He thought he wanted to capture a vaporetto turning into Canal Cannareggio. According to Paolo, the view on the easel showed the wrong side of the bridge, showing part of the railway station rather than the entrance to Canal Cannareggio. Sofia had tried very hard to hide her Venetian accent, saying nothing about herself but hoping she would be mistaken for a tourist; Paolo said very little. That man's Italian was good, but he was not fluent. Paolo thought he emphasised a German accent, but he spoke Italian like the Slovenian mother of one of their childhood friend.

Umberto took notes; he related his attempt to figure out who Bruno was, except that they only knew that he had a false US passport as Joshua Schwartz because that is what he used to check in a few months ago at his lodgings. He also established that he did not seem to have a job, but would appear every morning for breakfast. They suspected he was out most nights. His informant had overheard him discuss smuggling people out of Italy, and now his boss's boss had approved an official investigation into those operations. He now had the resources to follow all three men and had the co-operation of the police station at the port in Marghera. His assistant was investigating whether there was a Joseph Heber from Switzerland studying in Venice; he had already checked the Conservatory. Alex volunteered to go to the music shop on Monday to see if he could catch the man with the excuse of wanting to take up Violin again, since he did have lessons until he was fourteen. Roberto confirmed they had spoken with the real Joshua Schwartz and asked him to stop in Milan for one night before taking the train to Venice. Alvise would join him at the hotel where he was staying and bring him up to speed in a safe environment. They had private investigators watching over Leah and the countess, and would rather not have more to watch over him as well. The countess, Rachele, and Leah would meet them at the station in about a week.

Umberto suggested they book seats on the fast train to Venice early enough to tell him where they were, and he would join them in Padua. Just to be sure. His informant heard them mention Leah by name, and she was now considered a potential victim; they would also watch her.

Paolo and Sofia Mondani were intrigued. Paolo, Alvise, and Gabriele had been in the same primary school as Raffaele Mustaki, but not in the same year. Both husband and wife offered their help whenever they needed it. Umberto thanked them, but he added he already had a lot of unofficial civilian help and opened his arms to refer to everybody in the room. He paused for a moment, then added that, on second thoughts, he had so many that two more would not matter and looked at Rachele, who smiled.

As they were getting ready to leave, Dina knocked on the door and came in with a message.

"Rachele, Anita rang. She told me to tell you that Leah, Leo, and Mario are having ice cream at the Zattere with friends. You know where. Leah is staying for dinner, so you and Gabriele are supposed to collect all three of them. She invited the countess as well, but aunt Deborah declined, saying that she was happy that Leah had started socialising with her peers and did not want to spoil it. She was sure that Rachele and Gabriele would not mind walking her home. Anita also added that the guardian angel was staying for dinner, whatever that means."

Rachele was happy for Leah; it also gave her an excuse to relate the conversation to the countess without asking her to come to the office the following day.

The following morning, Rachele was in her office with her nephew Zvi Treves. He wanted his aunt to check a contract with an Austrian company written in German. Zvi knew all his mother's siblings were fluent in German and Rachele started studying Law when Trieste was still part of the Austrian Empire. He told his aunt he was prepared to pay. She had answered with what she thought was a joke about him wanting to have a lawyer-client confidential conversation.

Rachele had reached the third page of the contract, looked up and smiled at her nephew; she picked up the phone, dialled the receptionist extension and asked Diana to bring her the forms that a new client needed to sign. Zvi looked at his aunt with a serious face and asked her to keep what she was reading to herself; she was not supposed to share it with anybody, family or not.

They expected Diana, but Alex Modiano brought the forms. He was holding a newspaper and showed the front page to Zvi; it showed the headline 'Arab man found dead in a speedboat'.

"The man had a Lebanese passport on him. Yesterday morning, the taxi driver went to get his boat and found his body inside; the police suspects it is connected with what happened six months ago with the man who allegedly was a member of the Haganah."

He had been looking at Zvi all the time; once Alex stopped talking about the article in the paper, he looked at their aunt. Rachele told him to close the door; she waited for Alex to do it and sit next to Zvi; she said in a serious tone.

"Zvi, once you sign the form, I am your lawyer. What do you think of that poor man?"

Zvi signed the form in front of him in Italian and Hebrew characters. Put down the pen and looked at his cousin and then at his aunt.

"I have no idea, believe me. None whatsoever."

Chapter Eleven

August 1948

Two days later, Zvi Treves was at Venice port in Marghera. Three crates had arrived from Prague to be shipped to Haifa. He and another man were talking to a customs officer who had to sign that the agent of the recipient, who lived in the newly formed state of Israel, opened the crates just to check that they had the correct shipment. They were in transit. Zvi and his partner had inspected the content; the customs officer only made sure that they put back in the boxes what they had taken out. He did not check anything else, which was what Zvi hoped. He then sealed the crates and cleared the paperwork to be loaded on a ship due to sail for Haifa five days later. Both men spoke Italian to the customs officer; they both sounded almost locals, not from Venice but the Veneto area. Zvi was from Trieste and the other one, who used to be called Federico Teglio, was from Verona. Both moved to what had recently become the state of Israel in their very early teens.

Like Zvi, Federico had changed his name; he was now Zev ben Lavan, which meant wolf son of the white. Zvi preferred to call him Federico because he did not like how Zvi and Zev sounded. Zev/Federico was now the agent of Zim, the Israeli shipping line. They were about to leave the customs area when Zvi spotted the man he knew as Joshua Schwartz walking through the gate. He hid behind a lorry, and then he and Federico followed him from a distance. The two partners had worked together in the special forces of the British Army during the war. Zvi knew that the fake Joshua Schwartz had met him, so he let Federico take the lead. They saw him join two other men, then they boarded a ship that was loading cargo. In the background, Zvi took a note of the name of the vessel. He gestured to Federico that they should go back. He had an idea to find out the destination of the ship the fake Joshua Schwartz had boarded. On their way out, they stopped by the customs office. Zvi found the custom officer who had inspected his crates.

"We were taking a stroll around the port. Mr Teglio was pointing out some exotic ships when we noticed crates that looked like mine being placed near the *Santa Maria*."

The custom officer looked at a ledger with the list of ships in port.

"I doubt they were your crates. We took them to a bonded warehouse. However, I have time to check. The *Santa Maria* is due to sail for Spain in five days and then sail on to Venezuela. The ship that will take your crates to Haifa has not docked yet."

Zvi shook his head.

"Thank you very much. I am sure I looked at the wrong crates. It must be the heat. Maybe I need to stop at the café for some water."

The custom officer tried his best to be understanding.

"Don't worry, mistakes can happen, and it is always prudent to check."

He then walked around the counter.

"The bonded warehouse is on the way to the café. I'll come out with you and check, just to be sure."

Zvi thanked him. On the way to the warehouse, they talked about ships and the weather. Then the custom officer went inside and Zvi and Federico continued to the café. They bought soft drinks and drank them on their way out. Once they got to the gate, Federico looked at his watch.

"I should stay in the office for another half hour, but I don't mind leaving early. Do you want a lift across the *Ponte Della Libertà*?"

"Yes, please. I owe you a drink for that."

Zvi waited until they were inside the car.

"Federico, please keep an eye on the redhead we were following earlier. He uses a false name, and I need to figure out who he is."

Once Federico had dropped him at Piazzale Roma, Zvi took the vaporetto to Riva De Biasio. He thought his aunt's contact ought to know what he saw at the port. He did not want to disclose the real reason he was there, but he knew he could count on his aunt's discretion. Rachele reacted as he hoped. She called Umberto De Antoni and told him what he had just found out, including the ship's name, without specifying who saw it. Zvi gathered Umberto had not asked. He could only hear his aunt's side of the conversation, but he thought his aunt had not given any evasive answer. Rachele also shared with Alex and Franco what Zvi had just told her. At the end of the brief conversation, the three young men decided to have drinks together. They took the vaporetto to the other side of the Grand Canal and walked to Alex and Zvi's favourite bar on the Rio Della Sensa, two bridges away from the Ghetto. They were sitting outside sipping a Spritz, talking about the heat, and discussing a day at the beach when Franco stopped talking, put down his drink, looked around to see if somebody might hear him, and lowered his tone of voice.

"I think I know why you were at the port. You did not just buy old roasting machines for spare parts, did you?"

Alex looked at his younger friend, flabbergasted. They all thought that, but nobody had the guts to say it aloud until now.

"You do not expect me to answer, do you?"

Alex decided it was time to toast to a day at the beach, swimming in the sea, watching girls go by.

Rachele and the countess were having their weekly private meeting over coffee and cake. They sat inside; the clouds in the sky were very menacing; everybody hoped that the sky would deliver on the promises of rain and a respite from the oppressive heat. By now, they were regulars at the café at a time when it did not have many other customers. The waiter came with their usual order: coffee and two slices of the cake that Anna's patisserie delivered that day. Rachele was not sure whether they knew she was the mother of the owner of the bakery that was supplying the cakes; she not only knew what to expect but had taught Anna, her daughter, quite a few of the recipes she was using.

That morning, the countess had something in her mind. She did not have a piece of the cake when it arrived, which was unusual. She loved that cake each time she had it whenever she was a guest at Gabriele and Rachele's.

"I had two very challenging weeks; yesterday, Leah agreed to see Doctor Corinaldi. Her nightmares have become more frequent, but that is not all. She remembers things from her life in the camps when she wakes up. She was one of the young women the Nazis experimented on, and listening to her memories brings me down."

Rachele had just cut a piece of her slice of cake with the fork. She was about to eat it, but she stopped halfway between the plate and her mouth and put the cake down.

"What brings you down?"

"I keep thinking of the conversation she had with her mother, who pushed her forward when they were selecting young women because she was sure they would feed her at the laboratory. That is what she said, laboratory. They treated them like the rats doctors experimented on."

Rachele looked at nothing in particular for a few minutes, shook her head, taking control of her emotions before speaking.

"That must be awful for both of you; I thank the almighty every morning that we avoided deportation. Is Leah's memory coming back?"

The countess took a sip of water and looked at the cake, but answered her honorary niece first.

"I am not sure; it looks as if seeing that woman faint when we were walking to have dinner at Roberto's triggered some memories of her life in the camp."

"What about life before the camp?"

"She still says that Leah is the name the nurse in the allied hospital called her, but she has no memory of anything else. By the way, what did you discuss when you walked her home after she stayed to have dinner with Leo and Mario? She now calls you Aunt Rachele, as well."

Rachele felt relieved, happy for the opportunity to change the subject of the conversation away from Nazi Camps.

"She loved being around a family; she told me you asked her to call you Aunt Deborah, but she thinks of you as her grandmother. When Mario and Leo described a conversation they had with Fiamma, she thought of you. She was silent when we crossed the Rialto bridge; then, she asked us if she could call us Aunt Rachele and Uncle Gabriele like Mario does."

The countess had now decided it was appropriate to eat her slice of cake.

"It warms and breaks my heart to see her light up when we are in a family setting, either with my children or with any of you. It shows that she may not remember her family, but she remembers having had a warm family life. She has even conquered my daughter-in-law's heart, and Gina has been very withdrawn since she discovered what happened to her brother and his family."

Rachele hoped the conversation would move to the here and now; she was trying to think of World War II as little as possible. She felt very privileged that she could.

"I know how I felt when we found out about Emanuele and Gemma and my brother Ricardo and his family, but I cannot even imagine how it must have felt to find out that her brother and his family were still alive when they were thrown in a cave[1]. Can we please change the subject? "

Rachele shared with her honorary aunt the arrangements that Umberto De Antoni had suggested to ensure that the real Joshua Schwartz could slip into Venice unnoticed. They had decided to be extra careful after they realised that Bruno, i.e., the fake Joshua Schwartz, had people working with him and the inheritance was only one part of the story. Deborah Camerini had time to eat her slice of apricot cake. She smiled when she noticed she had cleared her plate by the time she had anything to say.

"Let me see if I understood. The policeman that looks like a young Gary Cooper... Umberto something ..."

"Umberto De Antoni, Vice-Commissario Umberto De Antoni."

"...well, Umberto has decided that Alvise will meet Joshua in Milan. They will take the fast train together; Umberto will board the train in Padua. I am not supposed to be at the station when they arrive; Joshua will appear at my home, somehow."

Rachele smiled at the sarcastic tone in which the countess ended her sentence, contrasting the almost dreamy voice she used when she mentioned Umberto looked like a young Gary Cooper.

It was late afternoon; Federico Teglio was sorting out several telex messages that had landed on his desk. He was looking outside the window, admiring the ship that had docked a few hours earlier. He had been the agent of Zim Shipping Lines for almost two years, and watching how a port came alive when a ship docks or sails away had not grown old. This one was larger than usual; he noticed the port officers and custom personnel leaving the vessel. He was just looking outside the window; his mind was miles away. He came down to earth when he noticed Bruno board the ship with another man. His special forces training kicked in; he moved to a position where he thought he could watch what they were up to without being seen from the outside. He tried to memorise as many details as he could of the man that had boarded the ship with the man Zvi told him he knew as Bruno. Half an hour later, he saw them leaving the ship with a blond man between them; he somehow assumed that the man was a passenger or crew member. The man with Bruno was scanning the quays as if he were a human radar. Federico had the gut feeling that they were trying to smuggle the blond man into the country and they were not going about it correctly, but he did not know whether he was right or wrong. He saw them get into a car and drive away, but was too far to see the number plates. He picked up the phone and dialled a number.

"If you see Zvi Treves, could you tell him that the white wolf wants to talk to him as soon as possible?"

The man on the other side of the call acknowledged the message, put down the phone, and walked out of his non-descriptive hardware and household goods shop along the Rio della Sensa. He crossed a bridge and walked past the café where Zvi was reading some paperwork. The cafe was Zvi's usual place of business whenever a shipment was waiting to leave Venice. The man stopped walking and did not acknowledge Zvi; he shook his head, said aloud how much of a fool he was to forget the parcel he was supposed to deliver and walked back to his shop. Zvi paid, got up, and walked home. His room in the Mendes household used to be Gabriele and Roberto's late father's study before the war; he had a desk and a phone. He picked it up and heard the dial tone; nobody else was using it. He called Federico.

"What's the problem?"

Federico reverted to the code they were using as part of the Special Forces of the British Army; he even spoke English.

"The bird we chased the other day has been back; this time, he was part of a small flock. Buy me a drink in an hour at Piazzale Roma, and I'll tell you more."

Zvi had forgotten to explain that he had no direct involvement with the man he had asked Federico to monitor a few days earlier. He liked his aunt and cousins and had grown to like the whole Mendes clan. Alex's reaction to Franco Cantoni's question showed that Alex and, probably,

Gabriele and Rachele had figured out that there was more to him being in Venice than the coffee roasting business, but had kept quiet. Helping them would not jeopardise his other operation. He rang the law firm, spoke to Diana, who was still replacing the receptionist, and told her to tell her parents he would join them for dinner that evening. He smiled at Diana's comment. Yes, he liked his cousins.

After dinner, Zvi had a private conversation with Rachele and Gabriele. Afterwards, Rachele called Umberto de Antoni. She apologised for the late hour and suggested he drop by the office on his way to the Questura the following morning. In a random serendipity case, Alex and Franco were early in the office that morning. When Umberto De Antoni arrived, they adjourned to the meeting room. Rachele made coffee and took out the pastries that Anna's bakery had just delivered, then took the tray to the meeting room overlooking the Grand Canal, excused herself, and went back to her office to retrieve the notepad with all her circles. She started the meeting by relating what her nephew Zvi had told her the previous evening, saying she had learned it from a reliable contact.

"Bruno, or whatever his name is, may have decided to impersonate Joshua Schwartz because the money from the inheritance could help fund whatever operation he and his teammates are running.".

Umberto realised Rachele still had doubts.

"Why 'may have decided'? Do you still have doubts about his involvement?"

Rachele looked at her coffee cup. When she realised it was empty, she poured herself some water to gain time and organised her thoughts.

"I think I am missing something. I am only interested in this for the sake of the safety of Leah and the real Joshua Schwartz. They should walk around Venice without bodyguards. "

She paused, gazing outside the window at the church on the other side of the Grand Canal.

"Also, they are watching our comings and goings from this office. That made it personal. I hope you will share with us whatever you have found. Of course, we will co-operate with the police in any way we can."

Umberto De Antoni felt he had to say something beyond thanking Rachele and her 'reliable contact'.

"So far, what the confidential informer told us, and your information, indicates a smuggling operation. We have not established the identity of Bruno/Joseph Heber/Joshua Schwartz, and we only know the first names of two of his teammates, Anton, and Herbert, assuming they are their real first names. We still do not know what they are smuggling and if they are smuggling into or out of Italy."

Franco had been quiet all along; he put down the pastry he was eating and said,

"Why Italy, why not Europe? Could Venice be an intermediate stop for things, or people, waiting to be smuggled out of Europe?"

Umberto was about to finish his coffee; he stopped for a few seconds, holding the cup with his mouth still open; then he closed his mouth, put down the cup, scratched his head, and turned to Rachele.

"I had not thought of that. By the way, you need to teach me the logic behind all those circles one of these days."

He stood up, thanked everybody for their help, thanked Rachele for coffee, told her to tell Anna that her pastries were fabulous, and left for the Questura.

On the vaporetto, he kept thinking of what Franco had said. Then the proverbial penny dropped. They should not reveal to the fake Joshua Schwartz they knew his real identity, at least not yet. He had to tell Alvise Cantoni that the real Joshua Schwartz had some shopping to do before leaving Milan two days later. They still had no clue how Bruno knew so much about the Schwartz family; he still did not know whether there was somebody in the Pesaro De Bonfili household who, intentionally or unintentionally, was passing on information.

When he was back at his desk, he rang Rachele; he thought he needed to talk to Countess Pesaro De Bonfili. Could she be there as well?

Umberto had asked the law firm to make sure the fake Joshua Schwartz was busy when he was supposed to join Alvise and the real Joshua Schwartz on the train to Venice at Padua station. Umberto was at the law firm briefing Alex Modiano.

"We think that it if the law firm invites Bruno, the fake Joshua Schwartz, it is unlikely that they will have somebody at the station when Alvise and Joshua arrive. However, we are not taking chances."

Alex was ready with his notebook open.

"What do you want me to do?"

"Keep him here at least until half an hour after the train is due to arrive. I'll call when I am in Padua to let you know whether there is a delay. Just to be on the safe side, it would be even better if you invite him for drinks afterwards somewhere far from the station and the Grand Canal."

Alex wrote the time when the train was due to arrive at Venice station on his notepad.

"I could take him through the list of assets. It is two pages. I will explain how we have separated those belonging to Sylvia Schwartz from those she inherited from her husband, Raffaele Mustaki, because he died three months earlier. The taxes in the second group will be higher. It will take at least two hours."

Umberto liked the idea.

"It will be long enough to allow us to leave from a side exit and take the real Joshua Schwartz to the Pesaro De Bonfili residence using a speedboat that looks like a regular taxi. Except a policeman will drive it and I have also organised a plainclothes police officer to meet us at the station. Two officers and I will be a large enough police escort to make sure the real Joshua Schwartz arrives safe and sound."

The countess wished she could have the energy to be excited. Leah had woken up twice screaming; her nightmares were getting more frequent. After each nightmare, she had to be calmed down and reassured back to sleep. Her housekeeper had forced her to take a nap when Leah was with one of her tutors early that afternoon. Still, the countess had to admit to herself that she was getting too old to cope with nights of interrupted sleep. Once her lesson was over, Leah told the housekeeper to wait for another hour before waking her up. She knew that the countess's bedtime ritual was quite extensive, and she needed time (in Deborah Camerini's words) 'to take off her face, and then put it back on again.' Leah insisted on taking the tray with coffee to her honorary aunt; after all, she had seen her 'without her face' in the middle of the night. She found her sitting at her dressing table, brushing her hair in front of a mirror. She put the tray down and sat on the bed, watching.

The countess could see Leah's face from her mirror. She kept brushing her hair.

"My daughter used to sit there with the same expression when she was a child. In those days, 'putting my face on' was much faster."

By now, Leah knew the countess well enough to know she had not finished. The countess stopped brushing her hair, still holding her hairbrush, shook her head, then continued brushing her hair.

"A shame Sarah did not learn from me. She is a very practical person who does not take care of herself well enough."

She turned to Leah, brandishing her hairbrush as if it were a weapon to reinforce what she was about to say.

"Appearance is important. When you are not in control or when you are not a hundred percent confident of your ability to get the result you want, knowing you look perfect helps. Never forget that you are as good as any man; Aunt Rachele's mother says that the difference lies with procreation, not cogitation. However, men take notice of a woman's appearance. A shabby-looking beautiful woman is almost invisible; a woman who is not very good-looking but takes care of herself and how she looks is never invisible. It will take you less time to earn people's respect if they see you."

She then went back to 'putting her face on.' Her honorary nephew Joshua was due to arrive, and she had to look perfect for him. Leah felt privileged to stay and look at a process that very few people were allowed to witness. When they emerged from the bedroom, Deborah Camerini looked very elegant, twenty years younger, and had the energy to be excited at her guest's arrival. When the doorbell rang, she was at the door; she opened it to find two familiar faces. Alvise

Cantoni and Umberto de Antoni and somebody wearing a large Panama hat, sunglasses, and a cache-col, looking like a film star from the nineteen-thirties. She did not expect that; her smiling face showed her perplexity for a few seconds until the young man took his sunglasses off, smiled, and hugged her, his words putting the excitement back into her face.

"Aunt Deborah, it is great to see you again. You look like I remember you from the last time we had dinner here twelve years ago before we left for the United States."

Alvise Cantoni watched the scene and noticed that contrary to the fake Joshua Schwartz, the real Joshua Schwartz spoke Italian without an American accent. He still spoke Italian like a local.

Chapter Twelve

August 1948

The barman of the café where Rachele and the countess met every other week, did not expect to see Rachele arrive with two men, something that had never happened before. One of them showed him his identification as a policeman and asked him if he could stop anybody else from entering the courtyard until they had finished. Only the countess (he referred to her as 'the lady who usually comes with Avvocato Modiano') and the two men with her could join them. He forgot to mention to the barman that the two young men playing cards at the table by the door were two plainclothes policemen. He was still talking to the barman when the countess appeared with the real Joshua Schwartz and Franco Cantoni. Shortly afterwards, a man came in; he ordered coffee and sat at a table outside the door as if he were waiting for somebody. The smile on the face of the others made Umberto De Antoni realise he was the private guardian angel of the countess. He looked past Franco Cantoni at the two men playing cards. When one of them looked up, he tilted his head towards the man sitting at the table outside and smiled. He hoped they would get the message. The same plainclothes policeman looked at the table where the bodyguard was sitting and smiled back. Umberto hoped he had figured it out; the man sitting outside by the door was not a threat.

The barman adjusted tables and chairs so six people could sit in the shade and have somewhere to put notepads, drinks, and plates. They all sat down and ordered. Joshua Schwartz removed his hat and sunglasses as they were waiting for their drinks.

"Freedom, at last. It almost feels as if I am wearing a mask. I do not think my mother would recognise me when I wear this hat and these sunglasses."

Franco Cantoni and Roberto Mendes saw him for the first time. They looked at each other; Franco spoke first.

"I can see why it was easier for Bruno, or whatever his name is, to impersonate you. You do not look alike, but your descriptions sort of match. You both have red hairs, grey eyes, and very light skin, and we can describe both as tall and slim with broad shoulders. You are taller, with broader shoulders, but you are almost interchangeable based on a description."

"Ok, so why is this masquerade necessary?"

Rachele and the countess looked at each other. Rachele looked at Umberto de Antoni as if to grant him permission to speak; after all, he was the policeman in the group. The Vice-Commissario said that the story started with the inheritance and the law firm, so Rachele started summarising the situation until she got to the conversation overheard by the confidential informer. At that point, Umberto continued, occasionally asking Rachele, Franco Cantoni, or Roberto Mendes to step in. Once the summary was over, he wanted to make sure that Joshua Schwartz had got the message.

"I hope you now appreciate why we asked you to hide your face, why we are not having this meeting at the law firm or the Pesaro De Bonfili residence. As Franco Cantoni put it a short while ago, you and the fake Joshua Schwartz do not look very similar, but anybody would describe you almost in the same way."

"i understand that, but I still do not understand the secrecy."

"We know Bruno, or whatever that person's name is, is not working alone. We are not sure who the boss is; it could be him, one of the others, or even somebody not in Venice."

Joshua started sipping his coffee, changed his mind, and put the cup down.

"Do you know what they do here in Venice?"

Umberto De Antoni put down his glass of water

"They may be implicated in an international smuggling operation and are trying to lay their hands on the Schwartz estate to fund it, or they might just be common criminals. We know they have tried to harm Leah three times and were talking about trying again. We are not sure what would happen if they thought you were here. That is why we ask you to go out with the hat covering your hair and the sunglasses until we know more."

Joshua Schwartz looked at the assembled company. He would not sit in the large Pesaro De Bonfili residence waiting for events.

"You said he plays the violin every Monday. What if, on Monday, Franco and I go to the café near the shop? Maybe I have met him before; I am intrigued to find out how and why he knows so much about my family."

The countess was enjoying sitting between her golden boy, Roberto Mendes, and the handsome honorary great-nephew, Jacob Schwartz. She felt she had to contribute something before leaving the group to collect Leah from the tutor.

"If you do that, maybe you should have protection like Leah and I have. I can fund it for the moment, and then Roberto and Rachele can figure out whether it is legal for the estate to refund me. I think I would like to go ahead with it. Roberto, can you organise it?"

She then stood up, kissed everybody on their forehead, including Umberto de Antoni (with a passing comment about the 'recent addition to her cavalry regiment'), and then left the courtyard. Her bodyguard left with her.

Rachele and Roberto were about to give Joshua a formal update on the recovery of seized assets and the issue of Leah's identity. Before they started, Joshua told them he was sure his father would fund the extra surveillance; he felt embarrassed needing it. After all, he had served in the US Army for five years; Umberto replied for the other three.

"I am sure you were not fighting alone. Think of the bodyguard as your teammate. Also, those three would have to face the wrath of Countess Pesaro De Bonfili if something happened to you. I am sure they know her well enough to try their best to avoid that experience if they can."

They were ready to leave the café. Rachele wanted to tip the barman, but he told her 'the other lady' had already tipped him. Umberto said to the two policemen to go with the man with the hat and sunglasses, one of them should walk with him, and the other should walk behind them.

Rachele, Roberto, and Franco did not want to return to the office together. They crossed the bridge into the Ghetto, and then they parted company. Rachele went to a vaporetto stop in Canal Cannareggio; Roberto and Franco walked to San Marcuola to catch the vaporetto that sailed along the Grand Canal. Gabriele was at the windows of the meeting room and noticed the vaporetto his wife was on turn into the Grand Canal; he also noticed somebody with an easel at the end of the Fondamenta opposite the office. He could not tell whether he was painting or watching the building where they were based.

Alex was sitting in the Papadopoli Garden with another man, an acquaintance of his cousin. When Zvi Treves introduced his acquaintance to his cousin and his aunt, he added nothing else; they assumed the young man was fluent in Italian because he had Italian parents. Rachele later described his accent as generic from Northern Italy. He claimed he was a student at Ca Foscari. They decided not to ask questions because they were not sure whether they could verify his answers. They just decided he would be another reliable source. He and Alex were sitting side by side, pretending o discuss a book.

A passer-by had to get very close to notice that the piece of paper on the open book was not a diagram but a hand-drawn map of the nearby area with a big asterisk pointing at the guest house where the fake Joshua Schwartz was staying. The two young men were not looking at the map. Alex was showing where Zvi Treves was sitting the first time they went to check under which name the hotel had registered the pretend heir to the Schwartz estate. Suddenly, Alex stopped talking. He saw a man who looked like the description of Herbert he had read many times. The man was approaching the guest house. Alex stood up, followed by the reliable source. They both adjourned to the café Alex was pointing out earlier. They sat down and ordered coffee. After a reasonably short time, Alex paid for coffee and gave half a dozen phone tokens to the reliable source, asking him to ring his aunt to tell her how long Herbert had spent inside the guesthouse; he also told him to use a 'discrete' payphone. He should not try to follow Herbert; his target was the fake Joshua Schwartz.

A few days later, Rachele was sitting in the blue sitting room with Joshua Schwartz. She had with her the notepad with all the circles. Leah and the countess had just left the room. Joshua figured out that his honorary great-aunt and Rachele had somehow discussed the matter and decided it would have been better if they had left her and Joshua alone. Rachele seemed to take her time eating a piece of the cake that had come with coffee. She then started from the beginning, explained her system of circles to get to the big picture and then figure out if any detail was missing. Then she came to the point, the reason behind her visit.

"We know that the fake Joshua Schwartz is also implicated in something else, but why impersonate you? I am not convinced that they need to get hold of the inheritance money to fund their operations."

Joshua was not sure he had understood Rachele's diagram. He had no memory of her before he moved to the United States, but in the short time he had been back in Venice, he already had figured out that she had a formidable brain.

"What makes you say that?"

"It is more of a gut feeling than an analysis because we are not sure what their operation is. They know a lot about your family; they even know that there is a possibility that 'your cousin Leah' might be somebody else. Although many people know about her memory loss, her other possible identity is only known to me, to a Rabbi in Northern Germany and the Geneva office of a Jewish agency."

"A cousin of my mother's closest friend in Boston runs that office. By the way, although we know of her, we do not know her situation beyond what you and Aunt Deborah have shared with us."

Rachele felt as if she were getting ready for an unexpected question of a key witness in court. She sipped her coffee, drank some of the lemon and mint drink the Pesaro De Bonfili's housekeeper had provided, and took a deep breath.

"Here is a thought that has crossed my mind as we were giving a mock update to the fake Joshua Schwartz yesterday afternoon. You do not look alike, but you look similar enough to confuse any witness."

"So I gather. I am curious to see him."

"Our honorary aunt tells me you look like your grandfather. I only saw a black-and-white photo taken at her wedding, but I can see the resemblance. Do you know anybody who would know how your grandfather behaved after his wife died when he was sixty with two grown-up children?"

Joshua put down the glass with the same drink Rachele was drinking

"Are you saying that the fake Joshua Schwartz and I could be related? Didn't you say that at the beginning, you did not know whether the inheritance would follow the Mustaki line or the Schwartz line?"

Rachele was ready for that. Her notepad was on the coffee table, open to a page full of interconnected circles.

"Yes, this is a nagging thought that has been with me for three days. Please hear me out because there are details that are not yet quite clear in my mind."

Rachele picked up her notepad and found the page with the notes she was looking for. She points to a specific circle.

"We establish that the inheritance must follow the Schwartz line; we find out that there is a possibility that Leah Mustaki is still alive, but the young woman who answers to that name has lost her memory, and there are doubts about her identity."

Rachele pointed to another circle.

"We write to your father, explaining the situation. He then writes back, telling us he sent you a letter sharing what we explained to him and included two powers of attorney. One if he is the heir and the other if Leah is the heir, stating that he is willing to adopt her and take her to Boston to her most immediate family. About two weeks later, the fake Joshua Schwartz shows up in Venice. In the past few months, he convinced several people who used to know your family before you moved to Boston twelve years ago."

Joshua straightened up his back

"But I never received the letter; I left Vienna two days after my father sent it and went straight to Boston. I wanted to come to Venice, but my fiancé in Boston was impatient to see me after five years. She was impatient to see me so she could tell me she was getting married to somebody else."

Rachele did not know the reason behind Joshua's decision to leave the US Army. She felt even more protective of the young man sitting next to her.

"I am sorry to hear that."

Joshua looked at nothing in particular, thinking of that conversation. He pulled himself together very quickly.

"I was not the first US military who was dumped, and I will most definitely not be the last."

Rachele noticed the sudden change in facial expression; for a moment he looked defenceless. Had he been a witness, it would have been the time to ask a provocative question. Since Joshua was not a witness, she did not want to sound antagonistic or patronising. She drank her tea before continuing.

"Do you see why I started thinking that there was something more? How could the fake Joshua Schwartz know so much about the Schwartz family? My nephew Zvi Treves said he remembered seeing you with your grandfather before he made aliyah. Zvi answered to the name of Conrad and he was twelve; you were two."

Joshua interrupted her

"I remember Zvi's grandfather very well. My grandfather used to take me to his favourite café more than once when we were visiting him in Trieste."

Rachele seldom enjoyed being interrupted, especially when the interruption did not provide useful information or raise a valid point.

"Anyway, the fake Joshua Schwartz was convincing enough. Zvi was only puzzled by his nervousness, but he described the right café. How did he know where your grandfather used to go? So, let me ask you again: Is somebody still alive somewhere in the world who could discuss your grandfather after your grandmother died? I promise you I shall not disclose it to your father without running it past you first."

Joshua stood up and walked around the room.

"This room has changed little since I used to play on a carpet under that window when I was a child."

Rachele smiled; she could tell somebody was buying time to think. She did not want to discourage that.

"My husband, Gabriele, has similar memories of this very room."

Joshua came to sit down near her as if he was about to reveal a family secret.

"Two things just came to my mind; one is one of my grandfather's professional friends, Doctor Matteo Giadrossi. He was much younger than my grandfather, but knew him well. He must be in his late sixties now, and may know something. I also remembered a strange comment my mother made when one of their friends in Boston suddenly fired his secretary. She wondered if it was the same reason that prompted my grandfather to fire his housekeeper. I was sixteen. I saw my parents exchange a smile, but I did not think of asking questions."

Rachele was taking notes.

"Do you mind if we try to get in touch with Doctor Matteo Giadrossi? My family lives in Trieste; I could ask them to look for his address and phone number."

"As they say in the United States, be my guest. There is one flaw in your gut feeling. How did the fake me find out that there was an inheritance? Whom did you contact to establish my late aunt's family tree?"

Rachele lifted her head from her notepad.

"Thank you for that. I shall make sure Franco and Alvise give me a list of those they contacted. Any of them could be the connection to the person pretending to be you. By the way, you said you were curious to see him. Weren't you supposed to go to the music shop near La Fenice to listen to the pretend you play the violin?"

"We go on Monday; Franco had something to do at his university and could not come with me. Aunt Deborah would rather tie me to a chair than let me leave her home alone!"

Davide and Paola were doing their summer holiday homework[1] sitting at the breakfast table, Mila was busy with a colouring book, and Anita was preparing dinner. It was the lull before the storm; soon, Leo and Michele would be back with their Bolaffi cousins and Leah. They had been to their usual ice-cream place at the Zattere, this time with the added attraction of the ships from the Italian Navy moored in the San Marco basin. They were all staying for dinner. She had just taken out of the oven the mushroom lasagne Anna had prepared in the morning when the doorbell rang. She told Davide, Paola, and Mila to behave if they wanted her to take them to see the warships the following day, muttered to herself, 'Here comes chaos', and went to open the door. 'Chaos' was less noisy than expected; something was bothering Leah and Gloria Bolaffi. They followed Leo and Michele into the large sitting room, where they knew they would find something to do or eat, waiting for dinner. Enrico stayed behind and asked Anita if he could call Aunt Deborah from a phone away from his cousins. Anita did not say anything, but Enrico felt compelled to explain.

"We were sitting at a table eating ice cream and watching the ships; Leo and Michele were too busy discussing the details of each ship to notice that Leah had stopped talking. Gloria elbowed me and pointed at Leah. She had the same expression our father has when he thinks of what happened to him at Bergen Belsen. We know what to do with our father, but we were not sure what to do with Leah."

Enrico's explanation turned Anita's puzzlement into concern.

"So, what did you do?"

"I changed my seat with Leo, who was unaware of what was happening. Gloria was ready to hug Leah if she started shaking or crying like our father. I asked her what was going on; she looked at me as if she was surprised to see me or be in Venice. She then told me she thought she saw somebody in the crowd who reminded her of a person wearing an SS uniform, but she could not remember more."

Anita started leading Enrico to the study, where he could talk on the phone without the others hearing what he was saying.

"Leah looked quieter than I expected, but she did not look distressed."

"It lasted ten minutes. Then one of Leo and Mario's schoolmates mentioned the group of Navy officers wearing white uniforms, which brought Leah back to the here and now. Her face relaxed, and Gloria relaxed. I need to tell Aunt Deborah. Dad has nightmares when he has these episodes."

Anita left Enrico in the study and told him not to touch anything; on her way to the kitchen, she made a mental note to discuss Michele Bolaffi's nightmares as soon as everybody else was in bed. She wondered whether anybody had ever mentioned them. After all, they were worried enough to stay in Venice in August to support Myriam and their children.

When Gabriele and Rachele arrived home, Anita shared what Enrico had told her. After dinner, Rachele took Enrico aside with an excuse; she asked him whether he could describe the man Leah saw. Unfortunately, Leah had not been more specific. While walking everybody home, Gabriele and Rachele did not discuss the two Italian Navy ships in the San Marco basin. They were concerned and wanted to avoid mentioning Leah's or Michele Bolaffi's nightmares. Rachele thought she would call her honorary aunt in the morning to enquire about Leah and see if she had remembered anything else.

Chapter Thirteen

August 1948

Vice-Commissario Umberto de Antoni was sitting at his desk at the headquarter of the Questura in Venice, a fan his only defence against a sweltering late August day. He had tried Rachele's circles' method, but he was still unsure whether they were smuggling out of Italy, into Italy, through Italy. If they were just a smuggling ring, how could Leah Mustaki, or the real Joshua Schwartz, be a threat? Why did Joseph Heber/Bruno/fake Joshua Schwartz feel the need to impersonate the son of the heir to the Schwartz estate? If it was an opportunistic decision, how did he get hold of the letter from Guido Schwartz? The office was dark, and the shutters were closed to keep the sun, and the heat, outside. Umberto could feel himself dozing off as he stared at all these circles drawn on a notepad. So far, they had been providing more questions than answers. Still, according to Rachele Modiano Mendes, that was their purpose, and he had every faith in the experience and, most of all, the brain of the woman he met as Rina Von Moden in 1944 when they were both in the Resistance. He decided to brave the heat and see if he could invite himself to coffee and pastry in her office. He picked up the phone; she was available. He told his assistant that he was at the Cantoni, Mendes, Modiano law firm to discuss a case, left their phone number in case of emergency, and walked out to get the vaporetto to Riva De Biasio.

~

He and Rachele were now in the meeting room overlooking the back because it was in the shade and, therefore, less hot. The usual coffee and pastry were supplemented by the Mendes family summer drink of choice, a mix of water, lemon juice, and mint that had spent at least 24 hours in the refrigerator. Umberto de Antoni's diagrams impressed Rachele. Ironically, they had reached the identical question in their assessment. The policeman turned to the lawyer, a question mark almost written on his facial expression. Rachele felt the jug filled with the lemon and mint drink, which was not cold enough. She called Diana, who was on her last day replacing the receptionist, asking her to bring another ice-cold jug from the fridge, and pointed at a specific circle.

"Let us assume for a moment they are smuggling people out of Italy; where do these people start their journey? Are they Italians or foreign? Why do they need to be smuggled out? Who is funding this operation?"

Umberto had not thought of the funding side of their operation.

"Why do you think the funding is important?"

"The funding might explain the connection with the Schwartz estate. My reliable source saw Bruno at the port twice; once he boarded a ship with people and came out alone, and the other time, he boarded the ship with somebody who looked like Herbert and they came back with a blond man. Both ships were sailing to South America."

136

"The destination of the ship makes me think they are smuggling out people involved with the Nazis. "

Rachele closed her notepad with the diagrams.

"Can you ask for help to follow Bruno, Herbert, and Anton and figure out whether they are smuggling out or in? I doubt that the Schwartz estate will authorise the cost of private investigators. "

Diana came in with the cold jug and retrieved the one that was not cold anymore. Rachele shared her theory that 'Bruno' had his reason to impersonate Joshua Schwartz, and his teammates were just helping. She added that the estate could fund that bit of investigation; the executor had agreed.

Joshua Schwartz and Franco Cantoni were sitting outside the café in the Campo near the Opera House. They had a full view of the music shop where Bruno, the fake Joshua Schwartz, played the violin every Monday. Joshua had the usual disguise of a large Panama hat and sunglasses; Franco was wearing a hat and sunglasses as well because Bruno had met him at the law firm's offices. The two young men were speaking English. They had decided that if they met any of Franco's friends or acquaintances, he would introduce Joshua as an American friend visiting Venice. Franco was also happy to practice his English.

They had been sitting there talking for almost an hour and moved from coffee to cold drinks. Franco had been telling Joshua how much he loved reading books written by Royal Air Force fighter pilots about the Battle of Britain. He thought they were the modern-day equivalent of medieval knights on horseback fighting each other wearing full armours. Suddenly, Franco put down his drink and told Joshua to look at '10 o'clock' Joshua said that the US army was using the same convention. He looked and stopped talking. After a few expletives that Franco had never heard, he said,

"I almost feel I saw a young version of my grandfather walk into that shop. If we are not related, it is an uncanny coincidence."

Joshua suggested they wait until Bruno had finished playing and left the shop. They would then go in with Joshua, not wearing a hat and sunglasses, and see how the lady inside the shop reacted. Franco was not keen on the idea; that was not what they had planned. Joshua saw the person who pretended to be him, and that was it. Franco went inside, asked to use the phone, and called Umberto De Antoni. Half an hour later, a plainclothes policeman greeted Franco Cantoni as if they had been close friends. It took a few minutes for Joshua to figure out that Franco's friend was a plainclothes policeman. He smiled and played along. The music stopped, and they heard people inside the shop applauding; about twenty minutes later, Bruno left with a massive grin. Obviously, he loved to play and loved the attention. They waited until more people had left the shop; they stood up, paid the bill, and walked into the shop. Joshua took his sunglasses off, then he took his hat off and asked the young woman behind the counter to point him to the area where he could look at Vivaldi's scores.

Meanwhile, as they had agreed, Franco was moving inside the shop, looking at instruments, and the plainclothes policeman was looking at classical music albums by the door. A middle-aged woman appeared from the back of the shop; she could only see Joshua's back.

"Joseph, did you forget anything?"

Franco and the plainclothes policeman turned to look at her. Joshua turned towards her.

"Oh, I am sorry. From the back, you look so much like the person playing the violin here a short while ago that I did not even notice you wear different clothes and Joseph would not have had time to change. How can I help?"

Joshua spoke English and turned to Franco as if he were asking for help. Franco was about to translate when the young woman replied in heavily accented English. She came out from behind the counter and fished out a score of Vivaldi's Four Seasons. She added Joshua was a better-looking version of Joseph. Joshua paid; the three young men left the shop.

Franco mentioned that he had to tell one of his bosses, meaning Rachele. Joshua said he would like to talk to her as well; after all, he was on active duty during the last year of the war. He saw action before getting a desk job in Vienna and was not afraid to be seen around. The plainclothes policeman thought about it and decided he would follow them, provided he could use the phone at the law firm to call his boss, Vice-Commissario De Antoni.

When they reached the Riva De Biasio stop, Franco noticed that there was nobody with an easel on the opposite side of the Grand Canal. He mentioned it to the policeman, who wondered if they were busy elsewhere. Once in the office, they waited until the policeman had finished his call and knocked at Rachele's door.

Once they were all seated, drank the coffee and ate the pastries, they related what happened at the music shop. The policeman added that Vice-Commissario De Antoni was going to check with the Port Authorities if any ship was sailing for South America in the next 48 hours. Rachele was taking notes; she leaned back in her chair, her hands joined with the two index fingers touching her lips. Franco smiled at the puzzled face of the other two and mouthed that she was thinking. After a few minutes, she sat upright, looked at her notes, fetched the notepad with her circles, and added a few notes. She looked first at Joshua Schwartz as if trying to remember something.

"Let me start with the last information you collected; nobody is watching our offices. That means it is all hands on deck. If Franco's intuition is correct and they are smuggling something, or somebody, through Italy, they are now moving the items they are smuggling into the area from wherever they started their journey. I will ask for my reliable contact to keep his eyes open."

When Rachele mentioned her reliable contact, Joshua looked at Franco who mouthed 'later'. Rachele did not miss the non-verbal exchange. She drank some of her iced coffee before continuing.

"I am more intrigued by Joshua's reaction to his impersonator. That would confirm that it is worth our time, and the estate's money, to contact Doctor Matteo Giadrossi. I need to call my brother in Trieste to see if there is a Matteo Giadrossi in the local phone directory. It might be as easy as that."

The policeman apologised for interrupting her train of thought.

"If they are so busy, why was the man impersonating Mr Schwartz at the music shop?"

"That is an excellent question. Maybe he is their leader and is not involved in the activities, or his involvement starts later today. I wish somebody had thought of having him followed. Maybe we should move our resources there rather than protecting the potential heirs."

She then picked up the phone and dialled a number. Once the polite opening greetings were over, she came to the point.

"Umberto, do you have time to discuss where we are? I have some ideas I would like to run past you. May I give your man a note with all the times I am available in the next three days, and you pick whatever time suits you? I am calling Trieste this afternoon, so the better options are tomorrow or the day after. I might have more information."

She then looked at the young policeman and smiled.

"By the way, thank you for sending somebody to protect Franco and Joshua. May I ask him to go with Joshua to the Pesaro De Bonfili residence on his way back?"

Rachele closed the conversation, took out a notepad, wrote a few dates and times, folded it in half, and gave it to the policeman. The three young men stood up; Joshua looked deep in thought. Instead of following the other two, he turned back to Rachele.

"What if I call my former Commanding Officer in Vienna and ask him who could have had access to the letter my father sent me and I never received because I had already left? That could be another way to figure out how my impersonator found out about the inheritance."

Rachele smiled, stood up, led him to the receptionist's desk, and said,

"Please organise a time when Joshua can come here and use one of the partner's offices to make a confidential phone call to a US Army office in Vienna."

She then turned back to Joshua.

"That was a brilliant idea, but please wear the hat and the sunglasses when you come here. I shall deal with Aunt Deborah."

She shook hands with the policeman and Joshua, asked Franco to find out if the Trieste phone directory listed Doctor Matteo Giadrossi, returned to her office, closed the door and dialled her father's home. She spent a few minutes with the family butler while somebody found out where her father was and whether he was available. When her father came to the phone, Rachele explained why she was calling from the office.

"I wonder if you could help me. Do you remember Itzhak Schwartz? Have you ever heard of Doctor Matteo Giadrossi?"

Her father sounded surprised but happy to share what he knew

"I remember Itzhak Schwartz very well. He used to sit two rows behind us in synagogue. The other name rings a bell, but I do not think I know him; maybe you should ask Michele."

Rachele took out her notepad.

"Do you remember how Itzhak Schwartz behaved after his wife died?"

"I remember him because we were both married to Esther. Your mother and his wife shared the same first name. Esther Cohen Schwartz was an excellent cook; she volunteered a lot of her time at the Jewish Community. Your mother's best line to drag me to an event was telling me that Esther Schwartz had baked the cakes. They were always worth whatever your mother wanted me to attend. When she died, Itzhak was lost. Well, at least for a couple of years. Then he started several relationships. He was in his late sixties, but there were rumours he had a child one year after his eldest grandson was born. His two children, a son and a daughter, lived in Venice. You should ask your honorary aunt; her husband was a very close friend of Itzhak. Anyway, there was a rumour that his child was born in Abbazia, where they had a holiday home. How do the Slav call it now?"

"Opatija, dad, was the mother of the baby a Slav?"

"That I can't tell you. Your mother could tell you whether the story is reliable or just unsubstantiated rumours. She always paid more attention to gossip than I ever did. If you need to find out more, talk to her or your aunt Deborah."

Rachele told her father she had enough information for the moment. They discussed family for a while; Baron Davide Modiano closed the conversation by saying that the great-grandchildren had arrived back from school. Rachele could hear her brother's grandchildren running into her parents' sitting room. She said goodbye to her father, a man who had been lucky enough to prioritise three generations of children. She had to talk to Doctor Matteo Giadrossi.

Chapter Fourteen

August 1948

Anna, Rachele's second daughter, had invited her mother and her honorary great-aunt to a tasting session. She had organised it in the café where the countess and Rachele had their conversations over coffee and cake every two weeks. Diana was helping her sister, asking guests what they had tasted and why and which cake or pastry they liked better. She noticed that her mother and honorary great-aunt were the only two guests who had braved the dark sky and sat in the courtyard despite the promise of rain. They were sitting at their regular table; each had a small tray with several small slices of different things, their usual coffee, and a glass of water. Rachele was eating a savoury tart with an unusual combination of aubergine, pistachio, and mint. A variation on a salad from a recipe introduced into the Modiano clan by her mother, Baroness Esther Coronel Modiano. The countess put down her glass of water,

"So, you talked to Matteo Giadrossi about Itzhak Schwartz. Why did you not come to me?"

Rachele waited until she swallowed the last piece of tart

"Somehow, I did not feel free to come and ask you to dish the dirt about one of your husband's closest friends. I did not even ask many questions to my parents beyond what they volunteered to tell me."

"Is this why you sent Alex to Trieste to look into Itzhak's will?"

Rachele's suggestion to the countess to try the pistachio and walnut cake was also an excuse to get Deborah Camerini to eat, to ensure she would not interrupt her for a few minutes.

"Joshua Schwartz and the young man impersonating him somehow look similar; that was why Bruno fooled several people in Venice, despite his fake American accent. When Franco told me about Joshua's reaction to seeing his impersonator, I wondered if those two were related. That might have explained why Bruno knew so much about the Schwartz family. I thought his doctor might have known something that Itzhahk Schwartz might have wanted to hide from his friends."

The countess put down the empty plate, used her napkin to remove the crumbs from her mouth, and drank her coffee.

"You must try the cake I have just eaten, but make sure you take a sip of coffee when you have its taste in your mouth. I will ask Anna to send me one cake a week; it is too good. Anyway, back to us. I understand that, and what do you hope to find in Trieste?"

"Matteo Giadrossi described Itzhahk's reaction to his wife's death as a period of mourning, followed by resignation, followed by merriment."

"I could have told you that my husband described him as the Merry Widower five years after his wife's death."

Rachele tried a piece of another tart before continuing.

"Well, he put me in touch with the son of his accountant, who has inherited his father's accounting practice. He was a young apprentice in the nineteen twenties, but he was pretty sure that there were regular monthly payments that were not to be considered when they were doing their clients' tax returns."

"You think there was an illegitimate child somewhere?"

"Well, I thought of a potential family connection. Joshua made me think of an illegitimate child when he told me that seeing Bruno for the first time was like seeing the man from the photographs of his paternal grandparents when they were young. Just to change the person. How is Leah? What does Joshua think of her?"

The countess looked at her empty tray.

"I wish we could call the waiter to get a refill, but I must not. Joshua agrees with us; whoever she is, she is not pretending. He has no direct recollection of his cousin. She was four when they left Italy. He pointed out that she is relaxed, leaving us alone. If she were pretending, she would want to know what we say to each other all the time."

"How is she doing with Doctor Corinaldi?"

"She is thrilled with her sessions, except the memories coming back are those of her life in the camps. She was one of many girls who were used for medical experiments. Something that is not nice to hear, but it saved her life. Doctor Corinaldi thinks her survivor's guilt is blocking any memory of life before the camp."

The countess paused and looked at Rachele, their unspoken exchange written in their faces. They did not like to think of the War. Deborah Camerini drank some water before continuing.

"Joshua thinks her happiness when she is in a large family setting means she is not Leah. Leah was an only child and only had four cousins. This Leah is very happy with a large extended family; my grandchildren call her aunt. She insists she is just Aunt, no name attached. I think she knows her memory is coming back, and she worries about changing how we call her and our feelings for her."

"I noticed she is reluctant to use names when she is with my lot. She is becoming very close to Leo and Mario and seems very relaxed around them. She is also very good with Mila; I wonder whether she had younger siblings."

They felt some raindrops, collected their handbags and trays and moved inside; they had barely gone through the door when it started raining.

Joshua Schwartz's former commanding officer, Colonel McLaren, had been very helpful. After their initial conversation, a sketch artist spent a couple of hours with Vice-Commissario De Antoni's confidential informer, the bartender in the café near the shipyard at Giudecca. Franco Cantoni recognised "Herbert" as the man who followed Leah and the countess. Paolo and Sofia Mondani confirmed that "Anton" was the man with the easel on the other side of the Grand Canal. Once the confidential informer approved the sketches, Joshua and the Vice-Commissario took them to a US base near Venice, following the Colonel's instructions. They had a phototelegraphy machine to send them to the Colonel in Vienna. Two days later, Joshua and Umberto De Antoni were in Rachele's office discussing the information provided by Colonel McLaren once he saw the sketches. Rachele had the notepad with all the circles on one side. As Joshua was talking, she was taking notes in a different scrapbook. Once Joshua had finished, Umberto looked at her with a question mark on his face. Rachele put the scrapbook back and picked up the notepad with the circles. She added some notes, checking the other notepad.

"We are making progress. I think we know how they found out about the inheritance; Herbert, whose full name is Herbert Platz, was part of the cleaning staff at Joshua's old office. He must have known that you would not come back, so, for whatever reason, he picked the letter that had been left on your old desk."

Joshua was annoyed.

"I saw the sketches. I should have recognised him."

Umberto tried reassured him

"It happens more often than you think. People do not make the connection when they do not expect to see a person in a specific environment."

Rachele smiled and continued with her summary

"We have made progress on what they are up to here in Venice. Thanks to Colonel McLaren, we know Anton is Ante Dragovich; the Yugoslavs are looking for him for his connections with the Ustasha[1]. Towards the end of the war, he fled to Vienna, where he used the name Anton Draeger; he might have been involved in smuggling Nazis and their families out of Austria and into South America. I wonder if they are doing the same here. I still cannot figure out their connection with Bruno, and I hope Alex finds something in Trieste besides his old bedroom."

Umberto had been taking notes as well.

"Franco may be right. They are smuggling people through Italy and out to South America. But why try to get rid of Leah? I would have thought it was in their best interest to be as invisible as possible; we must be missing something."

Rachele smiled, turned the notepad with the circles towards them, and pointed at one circle with her pen.

"We are missing the link with Bruno. Why did he feel the need to impersonate Joshua? I think it is the key to understanding why we are now worried over the safety of Leah and Joshua. By the way, I am not that relaxed over our safety either."

Umberto closed his notepad and stood up. Joshua was about to stand up when Rachele stopped him. Her nephew Zvi Treves was due to arrive in ten minutes. He wanted to meet Joshua, his Treves grandfather, and Itzhak Schwartz were very close friends. Zvi remembered meeting Joshua when he was twelve and Joshua two; they were with their grandfathers in a café in Trieste. Joshua had time and agreed to wait.

Zvi knocked at the door of Rachele's office about half an hour after Vice-Commissario de Antoni left. They moved to the meeting room where Joshua was waiting. Rachele stopped in the kitchen to make coffee; when she appeared with the tray, Zvi and Joshua were swapping memories of their grandfathers. Joshua had no memory of meeting Zvi, but he remembered Raffaele Treves very well.

Rachele put down the tray with the coffees, sat on one of the armchairs, and told the two young men to help themselves. Joshua noticed that there were no notepads.

"Zvi, I asked you to come this afternoon because I was hoping we could use one of your reliable contacts. I had no clear idea of what I needed to know when we spoke this morning; now I do."

"How can we help?"

"I am trying to figure out why the three men we know as Herbert, Anton, and Bruno tried to get rid of Leah. We now have more information, and it is still not clear. As you know, Alex is in Trieste following my idea of checking Itzhak

Schwartz's will, so here is where I need the help of your reliable contacts. Anton is Anton Draeger, who used to be called Ante Dragovich. He was involved with the Ustasha; the Americans know him as somebody who helped Nazis escape Europe."

Rachele handed a note to Zvi with names. Zvi looked at it, and there were two he had not heard.

"Who are Herbert Platz and Bruno... question mark?"

"Herbert Platz used to work as a cleaner at Joshua's old office; he may have told Bruno about the inheritance. Bruno is the name the bartender heard Herbert, and Anton using to refer to Joshua's impersonator."

Zvi did not make any promises but would discuss those names with his reliable sources. He knew his aunt knew that coffee roasting was not his only business venture, but had kept up with his story, and was very grateful to her and the rest of the family for it. He pocketed the note and invited Joshua to have a drink with him. Joshua accepted, and the two of them started walking towards the door. Rachele reminded Joshua to wear the hat and the sunglasses on their way out. Zvi made a comment about the world conspiracy of Jewish mothers, looked at his aunt, smiled, and winked. That gestures reassured Rachele that Zvi had at least an idea of what to do to find out the information she was after. Umberto de Antoni would be grateful to Zvi's reliable contacts. However, she was thankful she could knock at the door of Gabriele's office and walk home with him.

It had been a very mild evening. The mid-August rains had cooled the air and brought the first hint of Autumn. Venetians, worn out by the summer heat and humidity, had enjoyed the cool breeze coming from the Alps. It had been a great respite from feeling sticky all over. Joshua and his honorary aunt had been talking till late, sitting by the big window in the red sitting room overlooking the Grand Canal. The windows were open to let in the cool air of the evening; the lights were off to prevent unwanted visits from flies, bugs, and other undesirable guests. Joshua had shared the pain of the breakup for the first time. Deborah Camerini was reluctant to break the flow; she listened until long past midnight. It was past one o'clock by the time she had completed her bedtime routine and was in bed. It was still dark when somebody's screaming woke her up. She put her dressing gown on, checked herself in the mirror, and left her room, trying to figure out where the screams were coming from. When she realised they were coming from Leah's room, Joshua and her housekeeper had woken up and joined her outside. The housekeeper stopped Joshua from going in as well.

The countess found Leah sitting on her bed, crying; she did not say anything, sat next to her, and hugged her. Joshua opened the door, putting his head inside the room. The countess mouthed, 'later,' the housekeeper came with a tray with a bottle of water and a glass and left the room. Leah stopped crying.

"I think I remembered what happened before I fainted when the allied army arrived at the camp. I am not Leah Schwartz. My name is Elena Finci, and I was born in Rhodes. Leah and I had become very close friends at Birkenau. She was in the bed next to mine, and they were doing opposite things with us. I think they were trying to delay her first menstruation and bring mine forward. We spent most of our time sharing our lives before the camp. That is how I know Venice."

The countess kept hugging Leah/Elena, saying nothing. She just wanted to make her presence felt and hoped she could transmit love and support through her hug. Leah/Elena kept her head buried in her guardian's shoulder because she could not face looking at her.

"Leah revived me during the march and made sure I could walk; she was stronger. When we reached the new camp, they put us in the same room. They were doing different experiments, and Leah became progressively weaker. One morning we woke up and nobody was around, everybody had left. Leah was feeling very weak. Somebody shouted, 'they are here!' I got up and walked out of the room into the corridor; I was careful because we could not leave our rooms. When I saw an empty corridor, I went outside."

Leah/Elena stopped sobbing but was still crying. She lifted her face and looked at the countess.

"I saw a soldier. I wanted to ask him to get help for Leah. I wanted to say, 'Leah Mustaki needs help,' but I could not say it in English. I must have fainted after I said, 'Leah Mustaki.' Later, when I woke up at the hospital, I did not remember anything; a nurse called me Leah, and later, somebody who spoke Italian came to tell me that the girl in the room with me did not make it. "

Leah/Elena started crying again. She had barely breathed as she was talking.

Deborah Camerini had not stopped hugging her. She broke the hug, took the young woman's face into her hands, and hoped that her face showed all the love she felt for this young woman.

"You are safe here. I told you we all have grown to love you, whatever your name. My grandchildren adore you; Leo and Mario Mendes have become your close friends; you have become part of two large families, the Pesaro De Bonfilis and the Mendeses. Joshua was aware of your memory issues, and I am sure he will not change his mind about you."

Leah/Elena drank the water and stopped crying. The countess did not like her empty stare. She thought she'd better keep talking.

"Elena is a beautiful name; if I had had another daughter, I would have called her Elena. We need to do three things. Number 1, you need to understand very well that nobody here cares what your name is; they care about you. Number 2, as soon as it is polite to do so, I will call Rachele and ask her to sort out all the legal stuff under your name. Number 3, later this morning, I will call Doctor Corinaldi to make an urgent appointment. What happened is something that we had been expecting for weeks. It is a breakthrough, and you need her help. And, I forgot, Number 4, don't you dare stop calling me Aunt Deborah!"

The countess said the last line with the tone of voice she reserved for her business adversaries. Leah/Elena had heard that voice before. She smiled, dried her tears with her hands, and hugged her honorary aunt, who was now in full control of the situation.

"Do not use your hands; let me get you one of my tissues. You do not want to have puffed eyes for the rest of the day. Elena must look beautiful, proudly walking around Venice today."

The countess stood up; before she left the room, she turned back and said,

"Your friend Leah Mustaki gave all of us a great gift when she was dying. She gave you to us and us to you. She helped you up and revived you one last time."

The countess was going through many conflicting emotions, and had problems falling asleep. She left her bedroom and sat in one of the comfortable chairs in the red sitting room, the ones near the window overlooking the grand canal, and

waited for the sunrise. Leah/Elena had recovered her memory, all the doubts about her identity gone. Her future was waiting for her, and Deborah Camerini wanted to be part of her future. She meant it when she said that she was fond of her, whatever her name. She also realised she was grieving for Leah. The two opposite thoughts of grieving for Leah and being excited about Elena's progress kept her company until she fell asleep. The first ray of sunshine woke her up. She went back to her room. It was time to put her daytime face on and get dressed.

Around seven am, the phone rang unexpectedly early in the Mendes household. Aunt Anita was just coming back from the fish market. The phone ringing so early worried her, but she hoped somebody was in the kitchen, so she shouted 'telephone.' Leo and Mario were in the kitchen, ready for a morning of rowing with their cousin Enrico Bolaffi; Leo picked up the phone. By the time Anita walked into the kitchen with the shopping, Leo had already gone to fetch his mother. Mario told her that Aunt Deborah needed to talk to Aunt Rachele urgently. When Leo came back, he said that his mother had picked it up in the study, so Anita hung up the kitchen extension.

Rachele listened to her honorary aunt explain what happened during the night; she could reassure her.

"I knew that the number tattooed in her arms was registered as the number given to Elena Finci from Rhodes. So, all the paperwork was done with a view that Leah might turn out to be Elena."

"I am so relieved to hear that. Do you mind repeating it to Elena?"

Rachele knew she had to sound upbeat.

"Good morning, Elena; how do you feel?"

"Strangely rested, anxious. I was used to being Leah. Now I need to get reacquainted with Elena."

"Let me reassure you, Rabbi Lazar gave me your file, so I knew that Leah Mustaki might have been Elena Finci. So, when we petitioned the court in your name, we included your memory loss and two possible identities."

"So, I can stay in Venice…"

"Most definitely, you were born when Rhodes was under Italian rule, so you are an Italian citizen. We need to go to court to clarify your identity, but Aunt Deborah's guardianship already had a clause about your memory loss and two possible identities. It will be straightforward to sort it out. You are not going anywhere; we are not letting you go anywhere."

Rachele could hear Elena breathe a sigh of relief. She could almost sense the anxiety slowly leaving the teenager's body. Rachele made more reassuring noises until Elena finally spoke.

"I am beginning to feel at home here. I was afraid I had to leave."

"We won't let you go anywhere. I am sorry, but now I have to reassure the rest of the family. They are assembled in the kitchen worried or standing outside the study waiting. Either way, I have to take them out of their misery."

Nobody was standing outside the study; they were in the kitchen., and all looked up when they saw her.

"Leah remembered what happened in her last days at the camp. She remembered she is Elena Finci, and Leah Mustaki had died. It is tremendous progress, and we must all be happy for her. Details will be available after I get my first cup of coffee."

Vice-Commissario Umberto De Antoni was in a good mood. As he got off the bus at Piazzale Roma, he was looking forward to the coffee and pastries provided by the law firm. Rachele Modiano Mendes sounded almost upbeat the previous day. She said she wanted to coordinate actions with him now that it was official that Guido Schwartz was the heir to the estate. He was early and walked; it was a mild September morning. On his way to the law firm, he crossed the Papadopoli Gardens and wondered whether his boss would authorise a team of plainclothes agents to watch Bruno's lodgings. By the time he reached the law firm, he had reached the conclusion it was better to be sure of what that lot was up to before he asked. So far, he was investigating rumours. Therefore, he could not use too many resources, another reason to be grateful that the lawyers representing the Schwartz-Mustaki estate coordinated their investigations with him. Once he reached the Riva, he looked towards Ponte Degli Scalzi to see if the man with the easel was there; somehow, he was relieved he was not.

After coffee and breakfast, Rachele put away the tray and explained why she had asked Umberto to see her on his way to the office. She explained Leah had remembered what happened when the allied Army liberated the camp. She also remembered that she was Elena Finci and that the real Leah Mustaki died.

"We must tell Joshua Schwartz that his father is the legitimate heir. We have already told the real Joshua Schwartz, but I thought we ought to inform the fake Joshua Schwartz. Would you like to be somewhere in our office when we tell him?"

Umberto was aware Rachele's rhetorical question only had one answer. He said he would and would call later for arrangements.

Chapter Fifteen

September 1948

I t was a lovely September day, with all the memory of summer except for the temperature and the humidity. Rachele had finished her morning in court. The civil case was not difficult or complicated, and she felt confident. She was reluctant to return to the office, and decided to take the vaporetto from the stop near the Rialto bridge, not the closest one, but she thought it was a perfect day for a 'Canaletto moment', looking at Venice from the top of the Rialto bridge. She took her time to look at the Grand Canal towards San Marco. On her way to the vaporetto stop, she saw Elena Finci and her bodyguard crossing the bridge in the opposite direction. Elena was on her way to Doctor Corinaldi; she was doing much better. Now nice memories were coming back, like her home in Rhodes, her family, and her school. Rachele congratulated her and continued walking towards the vaporetto stop.

When the vaporetto arrived, she sat outside enjoying the day. She sat next to two German-speaking tourists who thought nobody could understand them. Rachele's fluent German meant she could and was both amused and annoyed at what they were saying. Then, one of them said something that made her think of something else, starting a chain of interconnecting thoughts that led her to one of the still unanswered question marks in the saga of the Mustaki-Schwartz estate. When Elena still had not recovered her memory, how did they know she was the 'fake daughter', i.e., not Leah Mustaki? She did not remember who said that; it was in her notes, but could one of them have recognised her from somewhere, and what would that somewhere be? She realised it could only be associated with deportation and the camps, so what if the attempt on her life had nothing to do with the inheritance but had more to do with trying to hide an unpleasant past? Like everybody in the extended Mendes clan, she had grown fond of Elena Finci; she had to solve that riddle even if it was on her own time. She had to discuss it with her honorary aunt the next time they met for coffee. When the vaporetto reached the Riva De Biasio stop, she rushed out, almost ran up the stairs, greeted the receptionist, and went to her office to look at her notes and all her circles.

Zvi Treves had finished inspecting three crates that had just arrived from Prague. The Italian customs officer had opened the lid, allowed him to look inside, confirm it was what he expected, and then closed the lid and put the seals reserved for goods in transit. They were supposed to be loaded on a ship due to sail for Haifa three days later; once the crates were loaded, customs would remove the seal. Zvi and Federico Teglio were having coffee in the office of the Israeli shipping line, and Federico had news for Zvi.

"When you told me the names of the three people I have been watching on your aunt's behalf, one of them sounded familiar. A couple of days ago, I saw them again around a ship with a Brazilian flag; then, it came to me. Ante Dragovich was one of the war criminals my brother-in-law mentioned they were looking for."

Zvi was sipping his coffee. He almost choked on it.

"You mean somebody called Ante Dragovich was in the SS?"

Federico Teglio stood up to get some water for Zvi.

"According to Joshua Schwartz's commanding officer, Ante Dragovich was a member of the Ustasha; we know that there were non-Germans in the SS; what if Ante Dragovich joined the SS and now he uses a different name to clean his past?"

Zvi realised he had just heard an important piece of the jigsaw puzzle Rachele was trying to put together.

"That is an interesting thought; I need to discuss it with my aunt."

Federico took the cup and saucer from Zvi, put them in the sink to be cleaned later, turned back to his former special force colleague

"My brother-in-law could also be interested in him; I'd better tell him."

Rachele had asked Vice-Commissario Umberto de Antoni and Doctor Corinaldi to join her and Countess Pesaro De Bonfili at the café. The last days of summer were an excellent excuse to enjoy sitting outside while they could. Umberto De Antoni's police credentials ensured that the barman did not let anybody else use the courtyard while they were there. As usual, the social chit-chat ended once they all had the first sip of coffee and the first taste of the cake or pastries they had ordered. Rachele sort of allowed the countess to think she was in charge of the meeting.

"I asked you all here while Leah, I mean Elena, is being tutored in Italian literature and history to discuss a possible recent development. It all started from Rachele's thought that when the Vice-Commissario's confidential informer heard them say 'the fake daughter', it was not because they knew a lot about the Mustaki family and the Mustaki-Schwartz estate. It was because they had recognised Elena Finci. Rachele figured out that if they had recognised her as Elena Finci, it could only be associated with the camps or the deportation from Rhodes; later, one of Rachele's reliable sources found out that the man we know as Anton was in the SS during the war."

Doctor Corinaldi, who lost a brother in the camps and escaped deportation herself, interrupted Deborah Camerini's flow.

"Isn't Anton a Croat?"

Rachele lifted her head from her notepad

"There were non-Germans in the SS, mostly ethnic Germans or from countries with strong Fascist movements. "

The countess took the interruption with good grace. She waited for a nod from Rachele before continuing.

"Vice-Commissario De Antoni asked me if he could show a sketch of Anton/Ante to Elena. Doctor Corinaldi, you are here because I wanted to discuss what it could mean to her. She remembers things at her own pace and is much less troubled now. She sees people her age thanks to Leo and Mario, and yesterday, she rolled up her sleeves for the first time since I met her, showing the number tattooed on her forearm. I would not agree to anything that might jeopardise this progress."

Vice-Commissario Umberto de Antoni knew better than antagonising the countess; he was formal, hoping that it would make it sound less personal.

"If Avvocato Modiano's[1] intuition is correct, the previous attempts at hurting Elena had nothing to do with the

Mustaki-Schwartz inheritance. They did not know that Elena had lost her memory; they just thought she was pretending to be somebody else to gain access to the money. Doctor Corinaldi confirms our perception that Elena's memory loss was real, so she was not pretending."

Doctor Corinaldi was about to say something, then she changed her mind and nodded. The Vice-Commissario continued.

"At least one of our three suspects thought Elena was somebody who had to be silenced. Why? Asking her would be the only way to find out. The problem is Elena may not be aware of what she saw even without considering her memory loss. The only way to take this forward is to show Elena sketches of the three men and see her reaction. I have agreed to this meeting because Doctor Corinaldi may help us figure out a way to do that without causing any distress to Elena."

Doctor Corinaldi had been eating her slice of a walnut and pistachio cake while listening to Vice-Commissario de Antoni. She took a sip of water and put down the glass. Her movements were slow and controlled to give her time to think and project authority.

"Elena is a bright young woman with an intense drive to live and an equally intense survivor's guilt. She feels she must live for herself and Leah Mustaki, and is coming to terms with the idea that she is the only survivor of her family of six. Elena knew she survived only because her mother pushed her forward when they were looking for young women for their medical experiments."

Umberto de Antoni's wife was pregnant. He shuddered at the thought of young girls used for experiments. Doctor Corinaldi noticed his reaction. She smiled at him and continued.

"Her bond with Leah Mustaki started there; their mothers pushed both girls to be selected for the medical experiments. She survived; Leah did not. When we started, she was recovering the memory of the camps; now, memories of her life in Rhodes are coming back. She is a strong person. She may not be too distressed if she has those she considers her new family around her."

Rachele and the countess were about to speak at the same time. They looked at each other and Rachele gestured to the countess to speak.

"How can we be around her to provide the maximum support possible?"

Doctor Corinaldi smiled; she had realised how much the countess, Rachele, and their families had invested in Leah / Elena. Her answer was straightforward.

"I think Aunt Deborah and Aunt Rachele should be there. Another person has also started coming up in her conversation, Aunt Sofia. I would also suggest planning some time with Leo and Mario after the event. She told me that being with them makes her feel like a normal person her age. She might need that afterwards."

Rachele felt she had to explain who "Aunt Sofia" was

"Aunt Sofia is my very close friend Sofia Mondani. She and her husband, Paolo, are honorary aunt and uncle for all the Mendes children. Elena might call her aunt because she heard Leo and Mario doing it. Maybe the best environment to show her the sketches is in a home she is comfortable with, in a room she likes."

Before Doctor Corinaldi could answer, the countess intervened

"What better place than her home? We shall have it in the blue room in my home. She loves it, everybody loves that room,"

Doctor Corinaldi's face almost lit up.

"That would be the best environment. I can see why Elena feels safe and secure in Venice. She has many people who care for her. I suggest that Aunt Rachele and Aunt Deborah explain everything to Elena before Vice-Commissario De Antoni arrives with the sketches. I think I'll leave it to you to decide whether Aunt Sofia should be there as well."

"Could you be there as well, Doctor Corinaldi?"

"Countess Pesaro De Bonfili, I cannot tell without my diary. Also, I am not sure I am needed. I'll be available on the phone afterwards and we'll decide with Elena whether she needs to see me urgently. Life has made her very strong, very resilient, but very vulnerable at the same time."

For once, Rachele had the last word:

"My daughter Diana is my part-time secretary. She will contact everybody to find a date and time when we are all available."

Alex had returned from Trieste. Gabriele and Rachele had invited him and Zvi to dinner the evening they were back in Venice. He and Zvi arrived with gifts for their cousins, from their grandparents. By the time he appeared in the office the following day carrying a small suitcase full of notes, they had already discussed the family side of his trip. Alex had invited his cousin to the meeting; Zvi had asked one of his Treves relatives living "on the other side of the border" to help.[2] They were in the meeting room facing the back; after coffee and pastries, Alex picked up the small suitcase, put it on the table, opened it, and took out the first notebook.

"Aunt Rachele, your intuition was half correct. There is a child, but it is a daughter. Itzhak Schwartz had done very well since his parents brought him to Trieste from what is now southern Poland, as we know from the sizeable list of assets that were part of his daughter's estate. He owned three houses and a hotel in Abbazia, now Opatija. One was the family beach home; two were an investment. He left all the houses to his daughter Angela Huckstep, who, at the time of his death, was living in the house next to the family holiday home with her mother, Anna Maria Huckstep."

Rachele was looking through her notes. That name had never come up before.

"Who is Anna Maria Huckstep?"

"According to Matteo Giadrossi, Anna Maria Huckstep was the housekeeper hired during the final years of Itzhak's wife. Angela Huckstep was born in 1927, making her three years younger than Joshua Schwartz, her nephew. The properties in Abbazia were a replacement for the monthly sums of money that Itzhak was sending them while he was alive. They received money for ten years and then received the three properties. He left the hotel to his other daughter, Sylvia Schwartz. We filed a petition to recover the hotel with the court in Trieste while we wait for a response from the Yugoslavians authorities."

Rachele updated the notepad with her circles as she was listening to Alex. The question in her mind was whether anybody knew what had happened to mother and daughter. She did not quite get to ask because Zvi took over.

"As you know, my Treves grandfather and Itzhak Schwartz were friends. I remembered seeing photos of my father and his siblings on the beach in Abbazia. I got a visa to visit my aunt Stella in Fiume, who remembers being a guest of the Schwartz when she was young. She and her husband had rented one of the houses before 1938, and her daughter Myriam and Angela were friends. Her daughter now lives in the United States. Aunt Stella wrote to her to find out whether they were still in touch. She rented a room in one of the houses last month, so she knows that the old owner, Anna Maria Huckstep, did not stay in Abbazia after the war, and the states seized the houses to be reassigned. The people who live there used to live in Mostar."

Rachele lifted her head from the notepad where she had been writing notes.

"There is a daughter, not a son."

She allowed herself to get excited. Her hunch was half right after all.

"I wonder if we can find a connection between the daughter and one of our three men. It is getting more and more like a riddle I must unravel."

Alex and Zvi were looking at each other. Neither of them had seen their aunt getting so excited. She felt she was on the right path to unravel the entire story. Rachele tried to control herself and speak in a matter-of-fact tone.

"What is the connection between Elena Finci and one of the three men? After all, they knew she was not Leah Mustaki before we did."

Rachele checked something in her diagrams.

"When did they decide to involve Bruno, or whatever his name is? Is there a connection with Anna Maria or Angela Huckstep?"

She wrote something near one of her diagrams.

"They were already in Venice for whatever reason that interests Vice-Commissario Umberto De Antoni. When did they decide to see if they could lay their hands on part of the inheritance? "

Alex had been taking some notes of his own

"Aunt Rachele, you also need to consider that if Anna Maria Huckstep is not in Abbazia anymore, they have lost all their assets, and they may be trying to replace what they have lost."

The conversation turned into family matters. Rachele asked her nephews whom they met and how they were.

Joshua Schwartz loved walking around Venice; he did not realise how much he missed it till he was back for the first time after the whole family emigrated to the United States in 1936 when he was twelve. Joshua loved Boston and enjoyed spending time in the holiday house the family had bought by the ocean in Maine a few months before Pearl Harbour, but Venice was different. He could almost breathe better and felt a sense of elation walking along a Fondamenta by a canal or crossing a bridge. The symbiotic relationship with water that many Venetians had was back. Giorgio Pesaro De Bonfili, Deborah's son, had just introduced him to a rower's club; it did not surprise him to find one of Rachele's sons and two of his cousins there. They had planned to take him rowing the following morning. He was thrilled, looking forward to being in the water the next day. The memories of the boat trips of his childhood were flooding back.

He was walking along a narrow Fondamenta, thinking of the calm water of the northern part of the lagoon. He was not concentrating on where he was going or where he was walking past. Somebody in a hurry bumped into him, hitting

166

his left shoulder; he lost his balance and fell down the steps. Thanks to the low tide, the bottom of the steps was wet but above water level. He stood up, but his left shoulder was hurting. His first thought was 'no rowing tomorrow,' two people in a boat full of crates joined those helping him get up and navigate the slippery steps. He was standing on his two feet, but he felt an intense pain in his left shoulder. He was close to the hospital. Those who helped him talked him into accepting a ride by the two boatmen. The hospital accident and emergency staff patched him up, and then he walked back to the Pesaro De Bonfili residence, stopping in a shop to buy a pair of trousers to replace those ripped by the fall.

Elena Finci saw him first; Deborah Camerini heard 'What happened to you?' and rushed out of her study, where she was negotiating the purchase of a few paintings. She looked at him, worried, despite his protestation that they had sorted the shoulder and the bandages were just a precaution for a few days. Joshua told her he had managed to buy new trousers and change into them without being helped, which did not reassure her. She kissed him, excused herself, and went back to the study, excused herself again with her guest, picked up the phone, and dialled a number.

"Could I speak to Vice-Commissario Umberto de Antoni? It is important."

Elena Finci felt very comfortable in the blue sitting room. It was the perfect place to have the 'difficult conversation'. Like many other young people before her, she loved that room. Countess Deborah's mother-in-law planned that room as a place for her family, where her children could play whenever they wanted to be with their parents.

In the following century, some things changed. The family had remodelled the room a few times. Still, it had always been loved by further generations of Pesaro De Bonfili's children and by all those other children considered part of the family. The countess had explained to Elena what would happen, and Elena asked if she could have Joshua, Leo, and Mario in the room and Aunt Rachele and Uncle Gabriele. She said she would tell them what happened, anyway; they might just be there while it happened.

Vice-Commissario De Antoni arrived and found Elena sitting on the sofa between Leo and Mario; the adults looked more nervous than her. After he explained what would happen, he started showing her the sketches. Her reaction to Bruno was that he looked like Joshua; when she saw Herbert, she asked whether he was the man Franco Cantoni saw following them. Things changed when she saw the sketch of Anton's face. She had a moment of very heavy breathing, clutched Leo and Mario's hands, closed her eyes, opened them again, and looked at the countess, who smiled; she then turned to Vice-Commissario De Antoni.

"The last one looks like the man who shot my brother, beat up my father, and later put us on those trains to the camps. He was a member of the SS. My father was trying to get us into Turkey, but we decided too late and could not find a place on the ferry. We did not have enough money to hire a fisherman to take us there, so we were all there when they came for us. My grandmother did not survive the days they kept us in old barracks near Lindos."

The countess and Rachele felt a maternal sense of pride towards this young woman who could tell that story without crying. Elena was trying very hard to control herself.

"When they put us on a cargo ship to mainland Greece, we were lucky; by the time we boarded, there was no room left, so we sat on the bridge surrounded by soldiers with machine guns aimed at us. There were only about fifty of us compared to the hundreds underneath. We were lucky; we could breathe. A couple of hours after we sailed from Rhodes, my brother decided to jump ship and attempt to swim to Turkey; he was sixteen then. An SS caught him by his ankles and stopped him from diving into the sea. He resisted, and they beat him until this blond SS came and shot him. It was unnecessary; they had already subdued him."

There was another pause. She continued clutching Leo and Mario's hands, the young men who had become her Venetian cousins. Everybody was silent, waiting for her to continue.

"The man was blond, and the details under the sketch say, brown hair, but it is easy to change hair colour, isn't it? The man shot my brother, then laughed and shouted that he would have his dive after all. He ordered two men who were also there to pick him up and throw the body overboard. At that point, my father tried to stop them. He wanted to bury his son somewhere once we had arrived on the mainland. The blond SS hit him with the handle of his gun. When my younger sister, who was only three, kicked him, he shot her as well. He told my father to be quiet and behave, put his gun near my temple, and ordered two other men to throw the small child overboard. He then turned to everybody sitting on the bridge, and there were only a few of us, speaking Italian, and told us to behave or else we would all go overboard. We were lucky that we could see the sky and breathe. Downstairs was so crowded that some people might be dead by the time we reached the mainland. Later, when we were loaded on the freight cart for our journey to the camps, he took my father away from my mother and me with the excuse that he had to separate men and women, but only our family was separated. Later, I learned they had put my father in the troublemakers wagon; they all died on the way to the camp. I never saw him again."

Elena had been calm throughout the tale; at the end, she stood up, ran to the countess, dropped to her knees, and started crying. Rachele, Gabriele, and Vice-Commissario de Antoni's first instinct was to hug her, but the countess was there first and was not letting go. Rachele stood up and gestured to Vice-Commissario De Antoni to join her by the window.

"Now we know why they knew she was not Leah Mustaki; we still do not know how they knew she was in Venice before we told her fake cousin. I wonder if Anton thinks Elena is one of the few people left alive who could recognise him."

Before Vice-Commissario De Antoni could say anything, Joshua Schwartz joined them.

"I need to inform my former commanding officer of this development. Colonel McLaren is in touch with the unit that is looking for war criminals. You may have the US Armed Forces help in this investigation, Vice-Commissario."

Meanwhile, the countess left Elena in the safe hands of uncle Gabriele and went to her study to call Doctor Corinaldi.

Chapter Sixteen

September 1948

It was a good day for the law firm. They had won a significant retainer from a factory near Treviso. They had negotiated a contract dispute out of court, and their client settled his bill there and then. Last, but by no means least, the last court case to recover the seized asset of the Mustaki-Schwartz estate had come to a successful conclusion. Now they could start the formal process of handing everything over to the heir or the representative of the heir. The whole firm had been celebrating. They had drunk the wine, eaten the food, and patted each other on the back, and now the three partners were discussing the next steps. Alvise, Roberto, and Rachele's conversation was a mixture of business and personal. They were discussing the forthcoming Jewish holidays. Alvise Cantoni and his family had been Gabriele and Rachele's very close friends for a long time. Alvise and Rachele worked together as clandestine paralegals for Rachele's old employer during Mussolini's racial laws. In those days, Roberto was busy with the family firm and clandestine anti-Fascist politics. They discussed who was hosting which meal and other matters related to the logistics associated with the holidays. Emma, Rachele's pregnant eldest daughter, was due to arrive from South America with her husband,.

The coming Jewish New Year marked the last opportunity for those Jews who had converted to Christianity to save their lives to come back, no questions asked. They were wondering who had not come back yet. After Alex and Franco Cantoni joined them, bringing coffee, they started discussing the next step for the Mustaki-Schwartz estate. Rachele had her notepads with all her circles; Alvise was the will specialist, so he summarised the situation.

"We are ready to start the process of gaining possession of the assets that were seized and, with the help of Gabriele, assess the inheritance tax. Our interesting dilemma is the fake heir. He still does not know we know. We need to discuss with Vice-Commissaro Umberto De Antoni what he wants us to do."

Rachele looked hesitant

"We need to inform Umberto that we are ready to start the next step on behalf of the estate and we still do not know how those three have all the information they have. Bruno may be a hired hand because he looks so much like Joshua, but they need to know it would be convenient for them to hire him."

Franco put down his coffee cup.

"Why is it relevant to the inheritance?"

"We need to be careful; we have too many question marks. I do not think we should let our guard down until we know what they are doing. We must assume they have attacked Elena and Joshua. Anton may even be a former SS. They have German-sounding names, but they speak Croatian amongst themselves."

Alvise closed his folder with all the inheritance details.

"How do we know they speak Croatian?"

Rachele managed to disguise she was very close to lose her patience.

"Vice Commissario De Antoni's confidential informer is an Italian refugee from Dalmatia, so he is bilingual and understands Croatian very well. I suggest I give a ring to Vice Commissario De Antoni and ask him if he can drop by tomorrow on his way to work."

Vice-Commissario Umberto de Antoni was sitting at his desk trying Rachele's method to clarify things in his head. He had been drawing circles for the last hour and was still struggling. There were so many question marks. The US Army issued a formal request to detain Anton Draeger or Ante Dragovich, whatever his real name was. He was sure that one of his accomplices, the one they knew as Herbert, had been trying to get rid of Elena Finci to stop her from identifying Anton/Ante, but had no objective evidence. He also did not know how they had found out about the inheritance and whether it was the inheritance that brought them to Venice, or they would have come to Venice anyway, and it was a nice add-on. There was also the nagging thought in his mind that they were too well informed on the movement of the countess and Elena Finci not to have an insider giving them information. He felt they were so close to putting all the pieces of the mosaic together and getting the complete picture, but something was still missing. Maybe the fake Joshua Schwartz, the man they knew as Bruno, could be persuaded to co-operate with them. When the phone rang, it was an interruption. It was also Rachele; he agreed to a meeting at the law firm the following morning, hoping that Rachele might also help him with those blessed circles.

The weather was still pleasant enough to enjoy being outside; September had not completely given in to Autumn. The sun had mellowed after the oppressive heat and humidity of the summer; walking towards the café to meet the countess, Rachele noticed a few brown leaves in a branch protruding from a wall. The light reflecting from the water was less aggressive; she was not wearing her sunglasses. She slowed her pace, crossing the bridge over the Rio Della Misericordia from the Ghetto. After twenty-seven years in Venice, she still loved the view of a canal from a bridge. She crossed the bridge and started walking faster; the countess did not like waiting for late arrivals.

They sat outside, saying it would be one of the last times before rain, fog, and colder weather took over. As usual, they kept the conversation very generic until the coffee and the cakes arrived. Aunt Deborah was an important member of the Mendes clan. They had meals and get-togethers to discuss; they were also eager that Leo and Mario included Elena in anything they planned to do with their friends. By now, the waiter knew to leave 'those two elegant ladies' alone once he had brought their orders. Today, he added a couple of new things they were planning to order. He wanted their opinion. Once the waiter was out of earshot, the countess had a very important question.

"Rachele, how complicated would it be to adopt Elena? How different it would be from being her legal guardian?"

Rachele stopped with the fork halfway between the plate and her mouth; she did not expect that. She put the fork and the plate down.

"Let us start with the second question. At the moment, you are her legal guardian; your legal relationship with her ends when she becomes of age. After that, you are just two adults and, from the legal point of view, your relationship would be like the one you have with Emma or Diana."

The countess put down the plate with 'the new thing' the waiter had brought them.

"So, once she becames of age, she may be an emotional part of the family, but, legally, she isn't."

"Exactly. If you adopt her, your legal mother-daughter relationship will not end once she becomes of age. It should not be complicated. Elena is a legal Italian citizen; she was born in Rhodes when it was under Italian rule. What does she think? What do Sarah and Giorgio think? After all, there would be another person to divide the estate when you decide to leave us all."

The countess had listened carefully. She picked up her coffee, took a sip, before reacting to what her honorary niece had just told her.

"Well, Sarah and Giorgio are all for it. They say their financial position is secure and they have no problems. Elena misses being part of a family. We were talking last night, and she told me she was happy she could borrow my family and yours. I want her to feel she belongs; I hate the idea she feels she is borrowing a family."

It was clear to Rachele that the countess felt strongly about adopting Elena. The countess took another sip of coffee before continuing.

"Giorgio and Sarah's children call her Aunt Elena. She is part of our family and her close bond with Leo and Mario makes her part of yours. As far as I know, there is no immediate family. She saw her sibling die; she knows her father died, and the Jewish agency in Geneva wrote to me they found evidence her mother and baby sister died the day they arrived at Birkenau. We, and I mean the Mendes and the Pesaro De Bonfili, are the only family she has now. Please start the paperwork."

Rachele took the notepad out and wrote an essential to-do list as the countess was sampling her half of the spinach tart; she made complimentary noises. Rachele closed the pad.

"Vice Commissario Umberto De Antoni will contact you sometime today or tomorrow. We have agreed that we shall act as if we did not know Bruno is pretending to be Joshua Schwartz and inform him that the estate has now gained possession of all the assets that had been seized. Umberto wants to see if he can convince the man we know as Bruno to become a witness. So far, we have circumstantial evidence on Herbert for attempting to cause harm to Elena, and we have her as a witness for Anton's (or Ante's) war crimes. Also, the evidence of what they are up to in Venice is circumstantial. Umberto needs him as a witness."

"And you think that you and your partners will convince him?"

"I hope that the threat of arrest will convince him. He is the only one for whom we have evidence of a minor crime, impersonating Joshua with the intent of committing fraud. I also agreed with Umberto that we shall represent him pro-bono. We decided that Alvise and the Vice-Commissario will play the strict and outraged legal professional. Roberto will be the pragmatic one, and I will be the understanding one."

"Isn't it obvious to leave the maternal role to you?"

"I drew the short straw. Roberto and Alvise did not feel comfortable being nice to somebody who was consorting with a war criminal. Vice-Commissario De Antoni also suggested that you, Elena, and Joshua be in another room, waiting to be summoned if necessary."

"How theatrical of him. I do not see Joshua or myself having a problem. Do you mind if I speak with Doctor Corinaldi about Elena? Speaking of Doctor Corinaldi, how is Paola?"

"You must check what Doctor Corinaldi thinks. Paola is doing great. Apparently, she asked Fiamma to show her photographs of her parents last week. It took her three years; I hope it will take Elena less time.

"Well, this is why I want to adopt her, to make sure she knows she now has a home."

"I think she does."

"Rationally maybe, but emotionally, she is borrowing. I do not want her to feel that way. As you know, my mother died when I was ten, and from that moment on, I borrowed Fiamma's mother whenever I missed mine. I know how it feels to borrow a family. When Fiamma's mother died, I was not one of the mourners, yet I grieved the loss of my second mother. It is different from feeling part of your family."

The countess drank some of the water that came with the coffee. She was not keen to talk about her feelings for the Mendes family, but she felt she had to.

"Our families are intertwined, but we are equal; each time I borrowed Fiamma's mother, I was acutely aware that I had lost mine. It is not nice, not nice at all. Elena has already suffered a lot. I want her to feel she belongs. Once I have adopted her, she will have her own family again; no more borrowing. Anyway, let us know when Joshua and I need to be there. Elena will come along if Doctor Corinaldi thinks it will not distress her too much."

Zvi Treves and Federico Teglio were discussing the schedule of future shipments of his 'coffee roasting equipment.' The Jewish High Holidays were getting closer, and they would disrupt the regular schedule. They wanted to take advantage of being able to sit in the early autumn sun. They were not in Federico Teglio's office but were sitting outside a café at

Venice commercial harbour. The café was near the entrance; they had chosen it because they figured out that the noise of road traffic would make their conversation difficult to overhear. There were a lot of ex-US Army trucks coming and going.

Zvi heard two men speaking Croatian when he was about to call the waiter to pay. One of the two men was a priest, and the other looked like Bruno, except he was not Bruno; he was green-eyed, shorter, and had dark blond hair. Zvi followed them inside, intending to talk to them; he wanted to figure out who they were.

Zvi found out who they were; he got more information than he expected. He now had to tell his aunt. She could now sort out some of the question marks she still had in her chart full of circles. He walked to the small Porto Marghera station, took the train to Venice Santa Lucia station and then the vaporetto to Riva De Biasio. Throughout the journey, he savoured his aunt's reaction to what he had just discovered. He ran up the stairs, greeted the receptionist, and told her he had to talk to his aunt. She would be most interested in what he had to say to her. Unfortunately, Rachele was in a meeting with a client and could not be disturbed, but he could wait in the meeting room facing the back. On his way there, Zvi bumped into his cousin and told him he had something exciting to share, and unless Alex had something urgent to do, he might be interested in listening to what he had to say to their aunt. His excitement was contagious, and Alex summoned Franco Cantoni; after all, he had spent as much time as he did on the Mustaki-Schwartz estate. When Rachele walked into the meeting room, Zvi stood up smiling and told her to get the notepad with all those circles. He had very intriguing and exciting information to share. Rachele went back to her office and fetched the pad. When she joined the others, she noticed that Alex and Franco were as excited as little boys waiting to open their birthday presents.

Chapter Seventeen

September 1948

It took time for Rachele to process what her nephew had told her. She shared what she knew with Vice-Commissario De Antoni early in her thought process and told him she was still thinking things through. and added that she might have drawn a different set of circles by the time they met.

It was the day of the meeting with Bruno, the fake Joshua Schwartz. Rachele had been too excited to sleep; she woke up almost as early as her daughter Anna, who insisted on being present when her team started baking, although she did not have to as the business owner. Anna could tell that her mother was very nervous. She suggested Rachele bake something to calm down, so when Anita walked into the kitchen about an hour later, she found Rachele, still in her nightgown, putting a batch of biscuits in the oven.

"Good morning. Do you have a difficult day in court? You only bake early in the morning when you are nervous or excited."

Rachele had not heard Anita come into the kitchen; luckily, the tray of raw biscuits was already in the oven; otherwise, quite a lot of them might have ended up on the floor. She greeted her housekeeper and confidante without turning around, closed the oven door, checked that the coffee was still warm, and poured Anita a cup.

"It is not an exciting day in court; today, we reveal to the fake Joshua Schwartz that we know he is Bruno Heber. We also introduce him to the real Joshua Schwartz. There will also be a discrete police presence. Vice-Commissario De Antoni hopes to turn him into a witness against the two other members of his group; whatever they are up to, one of them is a wanted war criminal."

Anita could tell Rachele was very excited

"It sounds thrilling, but may I suggest I look after the Kipferl in the oven, and you get dressed? Somehow, I doubt you will be as effective as you could be if you chair the meeting in your nightgown."

"How do you know I will chair the meeting?"

Anita started taking breakfast out.

"I have known you for 22 years; we have spent many a sleepless night in this kitchen trying to reassure each other. It makes a tremendous difference to be here to talk about something exciting that does not threaten our lives."

Rachele was already on her way to get dressed; she turned back to look at Anita.

"Indeed, although I would not be so sure about my life not being threatened."

In the end, Doctor Corinaldi had advised against Elena Finci's presence; Rachele had suggested that she and Diana might like to spend the morning with Anna Mendes, who was trying some new recipes for her business and needed tasters.

Vice-Commissario de Antoni thought he would escort the real Joshua Schwartz and the countess to the law firm. On the way to the law firm offices, Joshua teased the countess, trying to convince her that there was no real danger; they were just being careful. They arrived half an hour before Bruno was supposed to come; Umberto de Antoni was pleased to see that the two agents were already there. He had an idea how tall Bruno was, and he had selected two members of the police athletic team who were taller. The two athletic and handsome young men brightened up the mood of the countess, who smiled for the first time that day,

They had decided that the Vice-Commissario and the countess would be in the meeting room from the beginning. At the time during the meeting, Franco Cantoni would leave the room and come back with Joshua, followed by the two police officers, who would be ready to stop Bruno if he tried to leave the room or become violent. Everything was ready, including the two trays of refreshments and the drinks.

The fake Joshua Schwartz, also known as Bruno Heber, was on time; Alvise greeted him at the door and took him to the meeting room facing the Grand Canal. Rachele was sitting between her brother-in-law, Roberto Mendes, and her nephew, Alex Modiano, who was seated to Bruno's left. Vice Commissario-De Antoni sat sto Bruno's right with the countess sitting to his right, an empty chair next to her, and Franco Cantoni sitting next to the empty chair. Alvise was at the other end of the table from Bruno; they had already decided that he would open the meeting as if they did not know Bruno was not Joshua Schwartz.

"We have asked you to come here to inform you that all the assets seized by the Republic of Salò in early 1944 and located in Italy and the Free Territory of Trieste have been recovered for the Mustaki-Schwartz estate. The only one we did not recover was the hotel in Abbazia, a place now called Opatija and part of the territory of Yugoslavia. We were trying to contact the manager of the property before the war, Anna Maria Huckstep, with no success. Like many others, it is likely that she left the area after the war, and we do not know where she is."

Rachele, Alex Modiano, and Vice-Commissario De Antoni were watching Bruno. They knew he knew exactly where Anna Maria Huckstep lived. They also knew that Alvise was about to give Bruno the first hint that they knew he was not Joshua Schwartz.

"You are also here because we have important information to share with you. Both the executor of the wills, Countess Deborah Pesaro De Bonfili, and the primary heir, Guido Schwartz, have agreed to an amendment of the will that may interest you."

That was the hint for Franco Cantoni to leave the room and fetch the real Joshua Schwartz. Alvise kept talking in vague terms for the next three minutes. When Franco and Joshua joined the group, Bruno was as surprised as they expected. He tried to stand up, but Alex and Vice-Commissario De Antoni grabbed one arm each, stopping him. The two plainclothes agents entered the meeting room and placed themselves by the door, blocking the exit. It was now Rachele's turn to continue.

"Yes, we have known you were not Joshua Schwartz since Guido Schwartz sent us a letter to inform us of the arrival of his son a couple of weeks later, a month after we met you. When Joshua arrived, we noticed how much you looked like each other; if you are both in the same room, we can tell you apart, but most people could not tell whether they saw you or him. The logical explanation for this remarkable likeness was that you were related."

Rachele paused to survey the room. She had everybody's undivided attention, but she also noticed that Bruno seemed to be less tense.

"When I talked to my parents in Trieste, they told me that Joshua's grandfather was nicknamed the merry widower. I thought you could be his illegitimate child, so I sent Alex to Trieste to see if he could find some evidence. He told me that Joshua's grandfather had made provision in his will for a daughter, Angela Huckstep. That did not explain how you came into the picture until another nephew of mine bumped into somebody who looked like you, only with dark blond hair."

Bruno could not hide his surprise.

"Where did he meet my brother?"

This time, Rachele was not annoyed by the interruption. She almost expected it.

" Zvi met your brother and a priest at Venice commercial port. They were collecting goods sent by an American charity to help those in Displaced People camps. My nephew Zvi, whom I think you met, had a long chat with the priest. So, we know you are Bruno Heber; you were born in Graz to an Austrian father and an Italian mother. Your wife, Angela, and her mother, Anna Maria Huckstep, live in Trieste. We do not know how you ended up with your two teammates or whether there are more teammates, but Vice-Commissario Umberto De Antoni would like to talk to you about that."

Rachele looked at her honorary aunt, a silent question whether she wanted to continue. Deborah Camerini shook her head indicating that she'd rather not.

"Countess Pesaro De Bonfili and Guido Schwartz have agreed that there may be something for your wife, but that will depend on your conversation with the Vice-Commissario. The estate has also agreed to pay for your legal representation, subject to the same conversation. We have all agreed that it will happen here in the next room, and my brother-in-law, Robert Mendes, will be there to assist you if required."

Alex and Umberto realised Bruno had relaxed in the chair and took their hands off his arms. When Bruno spoke, there was no fake American accent.

"I agreed to work with Anton and Herbert to see if I could find something for my wife. Angela's father left something for them. They had a nice house and made a nice income from renting the other two houses to tourists. That stopped when the communist arrived in Abbazia. They were afraid because they were not Slav, and left at the first opportunity. They lost everything other than the cash they took with them and the content of three suitcases. Now we live in Trieste, and Anna Maria and Angela clean homes for a living. I thought I had a job with a charity helping people flee communism. Until a month ago, I did not know that I was helping former Croatian Nazis leave for South America. Vice-Commissario De Antoni, where can we talk?"

Roberto Mendes, Bruno Heber, Vice Commissario De Antoni, and the two police officers left the room. Joshua Schwartz broke the silence.

"He looks like me; I did not know I had a younger aunt. I wonder if aunt Sylvia knew and if my father found out when Aunt Deborah called him yesterday."

One of the two police officers came to ask Joshua to join the conversation in the other room to explain why the Americans wanted Anton in Austria.

For most of the meeting, the countess had remained silent, nodding whenever somebody mentioned 'the executor of the estate'. She had the last word.

"Now that we are sure who everybody is, let's hope they find a way to put the man who shot Elena's brother and sister behind bars. If what Bruno says is true, we still do not know how they found out about the inheritance or how they knew Bruno looked like Joshua."

Zvi Treves was in his aunt's office one last time. The family had organised a big dinner for him. It was the first time they had turned the big room on the ground floor that used to be the warehouse of the silk material into a large dining room. It was going to be a family gathering like the ones they used to have before the racial laws. Zvi and Rachele were discussing the business side of his trip. He had bought all the second-hand equipment he needed. The only thing left to do was to change the German contract to have Federico Teglio, under his Israeli name of Zev Ben Lavan, as the new agent. Once the business side was over, Zvi told his aunt about his last trip to Trieste to see his grandparents. He found his grandfather weak, but his grandmother was her usual self, the actual power behind her husband's life.

Dinner was the usual Mendes/Modiano big event; during his stay in Venice, Zvi had become an integral part of the Mendes clan, and some Modiano relatives had come from Trieste. Several family members had asked Alex what the actual business that had kept Zvi in Venice for the best part of six months was. Alex smiled and told them that Aunt Rachele knew everything, knowing that his aunt would not say anything because Zvi was a client, and therefore, any communication between them was privileged.

At the end of the meal, the countess stood up and thanked Zvi for everything he had done to contribute to finding out who the three men that had been threatening Joshua and Elena were. After that, Gabriele said the blessing, and everybody went home.

At the end of the evening, Joshua, Alex, and Franco Cantoni talked Zvi into a last farewell to Venice the following morning. They were going to have breakfast in a café on the Giudecca Island with a fantastic view of Venice. After all, Zvi was due to sail for Haifa in the late afternoon.

Rachele and Gabriele surprised Zvi at the café. They had come with presents for Rachele's sister and Zvi's small children. Rachele and Anna had also baked typical family cakes for Rosh Hashanah. Rachele joked that if they did not make it to Haifa, at least they would make his journey sweeter.

The late September afternoon was still warm enough for Leo, Mario, Enrico and Gloria Bolaffi, and Elena Finci to sit outside at their favourite ice cream place at the Zattere. They were talking about the last days of freedom before schools started again. Elena was telling them she hoped to join them the following school year; she was working hard to prepare for the equivalence exam in September 1949. The conversation turned to plans to meet at Leo and Mario's home on the afternoon of the second day of Rosh Hashanah. Gloria said she was looking forward to the refreshments when Enrico noticed a change in Elena's demeanour. Suddenly, she looked tense. Leo also noticed it; he asked her what the matter was, and Elena whispered she saw the man that reminded her of somebody with an SS uniform again. This time Leo stood up, went inside, and asked to use the phone. He called his mother and explained what had happened. Rachele told him she would ring Umberto De Antoni and send Alex and Franco to the ice cream place. They should not move until they get there.

Leo returned and shared with the other what his mother had told him; the atmosphere had somehow changed. They moved Elena to the corner where she was sitting with the back to the banister, a safer position; they thought it was unlikely that any harm might come from the water. When Alex and Franco arrived, they told her that a police officer would come to escort Elena home, but Rachele had suggested they all did. This time, Elena felt safe enough to describe the person she saw. Tall, blond, with light brown trousers, a white shirt, and holding a Panama hat in his hands.

~

Joshua was right; Colonel McLaren welcomed the news that Ante Dragovich/Anton Draeger was in Venice and that they had a witness who could place him in the SS and had been responsible for war crimes. He had travelled to Venice as soon as he could and asked that Joshua work as his interpreter and liaison officer. He had arrived from Vienna on the overnight train and had organised a meeting with Umberto De Antoni and Joshua in the afternoon. It took a few hours to update him. After the Vice-Commissario left, Joshua stayed for another hour to catch up with his former commanding officer.

It was a late September evening; the weather made walking around Venice a series of picture postcard moments. The Colonel's hotel was near La Fenice theatre. Joshua loved the atmosphere of Venice in the final moments of daylight before dark; he knew he would keep Aunt Deborah and Elena waiting for dinner but thought he could get away with it. He was sure his honorary aunt would understand that he could not cut short his visit with Colonel McLaren. The streets were almost empty; it was dinnertime. Joshua had reacquainted himself with Venice; the inner navigation system that allows many Venetians to walk around the city following a mental map allowed him to walk to his temporary Venetian home while his mind was full of past and recent memories. He was paying only moderate attention to his surroundings. A tall man was following him from a distance. Joshua's red hair made him distinctive even in the poorly lit Venetian streets. His shadow was wearing a raincoat and a hat, his coat was hiding his body, and the dark fedora was hiding his blond hair. If Joshua had noticed him, he would not have been able to give a detailed description. Joshua thought he loved being in Venice so much that he was in no hurry to go back to

Boston. He was free to choose his future life, the freedom his ex-fiancée gave him when she married somebody else. He wished her well. He was walking with his hands in his trousers pockets, lost in his thoughts. When he reached the bridge over the Rio dei Santi Apostoli, something triggered a childhood memory; somebody lived nearby; Joshua could not remember whether it was a friend of his parents, a relative, or a schoolmate. He was not paying attention to what was happening around him; the road was empty. His shadow saw it as the opportunity to act. Joshua was walking down the steps of the bridge; he did not hear or ignored the noise of steps behind him; the blow to the back of his head was masterfully administered. He fell and hit his head on the corner of a step. The blow, the fall, and banging his head on a slab of Istria stone made him unconscious. His attacker picked him up and threw him over the bridge.

The countess and Elena were in the smaller sitting room, the one with blue upholstery. The countess was trying to divert Elena's attention from what happened earlier that day at the Zattere that distressed her so much.

"Elena, do you like learning with tutors?"

"I love it. It gives me a sense of normality. I can't wait to start school next year, after I pass the equivalence exam. Maybe I will be in the same class as Leo and Mario. Did you know they started introducing me to their friends as their cousin?"

Elena did not seem to be distressed any more. The countess was happy her ploy had worked.

"Many people know that Gabriele and Rachele have family connections with Greece, which explains why nobody questioned that Leo and Mario have a cousin born in Rhodes."

A long silence followed. Elena was in her world. Mindful of the advice of Doctor Corinaldi, the countess left her there. She was ready to react to any sign of distress but was patiently waiting for Elena to speak.

"Leah and I looked after one another from the moment we found ourselves next to each other in the hospital that was a research lab. They were doing different therapies on us; hers made her feel poorly. I made sure she ate and drank; I was afraid they would take her away. We talked a lot, and I knew about her life in Venice, and she knew about my life in Rhodes. I now have children who call me aunt, I have gained cousins, and I have a big sister and a big brother. I think of all of you as Leah's inheritance. It is what I wanted; I am happy that Joshua's father gets all the money. I have a family again."

Deborah Camerini noticed Elena was smiling. Rachele was right; Doctor Corinaldi was very good. Elena had grown less anxious and more serene in just a few weeks. She was sure Elena still had her nightmares, but she was making progress.

They were waiting for Joshua to come home to have dinner. Hearing the doorbell startled them, Joshua would have let himself in with his set of keys. The countess smiled when she heard her housekeeper talk to Gabriele and Rachele. Her smile faded when they walked into the room with sombre faces. Rachele sat between the countess and Elena; Gabriele stood before them.

"It's Joshua. He left the hotel where Colonel McLaren was staying an hour after Umberto de Antoni. Something happened because he was found unconscious by a taxi driver trying to unload passengers by the steps near the bridge across the Rio Santi Apostoli. He is at the hospital still unconscious; Paolo Mondani was at the Ambulance quay when they brought him in and recognised him. He called us; we have been at the hospital."

The countess was very worried.

"How is he?"

Gabriele tried to be as reassuring as he could, but he also did not want to make the situation sound better than it was.

"He was hit in the head from behind. Somebody must have tried to throw him into the canal, but they missed. He has a lot of bruises and is still unconscious. When he wakes up, they will do all the tests to check; for the moment, his vital signs seem all right. The policeman at the hospital wondered if it was a robbery gone wrong. Joshua did not have his wallet."

Elena was crying; she said in a very low voice

"Joshua forgot his wallet. He called right after lunch to check that he had left it in his room; it is on his bedside table."

The countess forgot about dinner; she got up and rang for the housekeeper.

"Set aside the food for another time. Elena will have dinner at Gabriele and Rachele's; she needs to be with her cousins. I am off to the hospital; I want to be there when Joshua wakes up. It may take a long time. Maybe you should pack something I can eat there."

Chapter Eighteen

October 1948

The synagogue service for the Jewish New Year 5709 (1948-1949) was significant for the whole Jewish community. It was the deadline decided by the Rabbinical Council of Italy for those who had converted to Catholicism to escape Mussolini's racial laws[1] and, later, the threat of deportation to re-join the Jewish community, no questions asked.

Venice synagogues were packed; those who had endured racial laws and, later, hiding were curious to see who would show up among those who had not yet returned. Extended families who attended different synagogues met at the Campo del Ghetto Novo to discuss who was there. Franco Cantoni and a pregnant Emma Mendes Sonnino were discussing people who had stopped talking to them in 1939 and now were greeting them like long-lost friends. Roberto Mendes and Giorgio Pesaro De Bonfili were engaged in a similar conversation when Giorgio saw a childhood friend who had come to Venice to celebrate the holidays with his parents. He introduced Cesare Abulafia to Roberto; when Elena walked past with Leo and Mario, he stopped her.

"Cesare, meet my new younger sister, Elena Finci. My mother adopted her; in reality, we all did. My children, my nephew, and my niece started calling her aunt long before she became their aunt. She is from Rhodes. Elena, Cesare's wife Estelle, was born in Rhodes, although her family moved to Rome in the early thirties."

Elena made the usual polite noises, but her face was still beaming as a reaction to being referred to as 'Giorgio's new younger sister.' She exchanged a few words with Estelle and Cesare, then excused herself and joined Leo, Mario, and a group of teenagers.

The countess and Fiamma were watching the scene.

"Deborah, Elena looks very relaxed."

"Seeing Doctor Corinaldi helped her a lot."

Fiamma saw Doctor Corinaldi and stopped her.

"Doctor Corinaldi, *Shanah Tovah*[2], you have done a marvellous job with Elena."

Doctor Corinaldi felt she had to explain that the reality was not as good as it looked.

"Elena stands between Leo and Mario; they are her anchors. She feels safe with them and looks relaxed when engaging with others. She is always between two people she considers her world, somebody from the Pesaro De Bonfili family or somebody from the Mendes family. Elena is not ready to let go of her anchors; although now she has an extended family to belong to, she is still afraid of losing you."

Doctor Corinaldi excused herself and joined her family. The countess was now looking at her other protégé, Joshua Schwartz, talking to Anna Mendes, Alex Modiano, and her daughter Sarah. The hospital had shaved and bandaged his head. They were too far, and she could not hear what they were saying.

Suddenly, Alex moved toward Elena and the other teenagers. Sarah stopped Joshua from going anywhere, and Anna ran to Roberto Mendes, who was talking to Roberto Sonnino. Deborah Camerini's recollection of what happened next was something that almost happened in slow motion. Alex shouted,

"Franco, Elena."

Franco Cantoni stopped talking to Emma and ran towards Elena Finci. Leo and Mario had moved Elena inside a circle of teenagers. Still running towards Elena, Alex shouted,

"Roberto, Herbert."

Sarah was holding Joshua Schwartz's arm, stopping him from moving. Rachele had joined her. Roberto Mendes ran after a man, trying to make it to the bridge over Rio Della Misericordia. Herbert was running faster than Roberto Mendes; he made it across the bridge and disappeared in one of the narrow streets off Fondamenta Ormesini. Roberto Mendes came back empty-handed. They were all now the centre of attention. Alex was explaining to Rachele, Gabriele, and the countess that he saw somebody who looked like the sketch of Herbert moving towards Elena, Franco Cantoni, who was the only one to have seen Herbert in real life, confirmed that it was indeed Herbert. The countess ran towards Elena, hugged her, and hugged Leo and Mario, thanking them for protecting her daughter. People started leaving the campo; Gabriele and Rachele had invited the countess, Elena, and Joshua to lunch. On their way to Campo San Giacomo dall'Orio, Elena Finci surprised the countess and Rachele.

"I think they know I am a threat; Joshua explained I am one of the few witnesses who could recognise the man who calls himself Anton as a former SS and a war criminal. I am not afraid; I will tell Joshua to tell the American colonel I am ready to do whatever it takes to help. It is my turn to fight."

Rachele and the countess looked at each other. They had never heard Elena sound so determined.

~

On the second day of Rosh Hashanah, after lunch, Gabriele had picked up his father's tradition and gathered the Venetian Mendes cousins to tell them some family stories of time past. This year was also the opportunity to mark the beginning of the school year. Enrico would start his final year of high school. Leo, Mario, and Gloria were in their third year out of five, Davide and Paola were in middle school, and Milla would start nursery. They could not leave Elena out. Given what happened the previous day in the Campo del Ghetto Novo, the countess was reluctant to let Elena walk alone to Campo San Giacomo dall'Orio. Joshua had still not recovered after his attack, so Alex Modiano and Franco Cantoni offered to escort Elena. They wanted to spend time with Emma and her husband, so they were also going to Gabriele and Rachele's home.

Elena enjoyed the afternoon; Leo and Mario decided to walk her home. Rachele suggested that Alex and Franco go with them. When they were about to cross the Ponte Degli Scalzi, Franco noticed Herbert sitting at a café with another gentleman. He caught Alex's attention and pointed towards Herbert with his head. They placed themselves on each side of Elena. Leo figured out what they were doing and suggested to Mario they ought to walk behind her. Alex and Franco made a mental note to discuss it with Rachele and Gabriele the following day; they might not have figured out where they lived, but they had figured out on which side of the Grand Canal they lived.

Herbert might have just been waiting for somebody to arrive either by train or by road. They were about to turn into the narrow alleyway where the entrance to the building where he countess, Elena, and Joshua lived was located, when Elena mentioned to Alex that she had just seen the blond man that reminded her of somebody in an SS uniform. Leo overheard her and asked if it was the same man she had seen a few days earlier. Elena's answer worried Alex and Franco.

"I think so. I wonder whether he follows me."

Alex asked them to wait in the alleyway and retraced his step to Strada Nuova and acted as if he had to pick something from the street. He wanted to look at the blond man, describe him to Joshua, and to a police sketch artist the following morning. Was the blond man following Elena or Joshua, pretending he was one of the several tourists walking around Venice?

Vice-Commissario Umberto De Antoni invited himself for coffee a few days after Rosh Hashanah; he hoped talking to Rachele might help him clarify what to do next. The first foggy day had come early. The fog made everything look out of focus, almost like an impressionist painting. It was a cold day for October, but he sat outside for the brief journey on the vaporetto wondering whether his wife would ever agree to move to 'Venice proper' from the mainland and become 'Venetian of the water' instead of being adopted 'Venetians of the land' as they were now[3]. The day was very humid, the sort of humidity that gets into your bones irrespective of the temperature or any ache.

He climbed the stairs to the Law firm's office two steps at a time. Umberto was looking forward to a hot drink. The receptionist was at the door.

"Good morning, Vice-Commissario."

The warm temperature pleasantly surprised Umberto.

"Good morning. The office feels very nice today."

"We have the heating on low. It makes the office feel less humid. Avvocato Modiano is waiting for you in the kitchen."

Rachele came out of the kitchen to greet him.

"I thought hot chocolate would be better than coffee, given the day. Gabriele and I needed to feel warm inside after the short walk from home. I can make you a coffee if you like."

Umberto grabbed the hot cup with both hands and let the warmth flow through his body. He was eager to pick Rachele's brain, so they started the conversation in the kitchen; Gabriele excused himself, claiming he had to call clients that had not paid their bills yet. Alex came in to make himself a coffee; Rachele decided it was better to talk in her office. They put some pastries and the two cups of hot chocolate on a tray and moved. Once they were in her office, Rachele summarised what they had discussed in the kitchen.

"So, Bruno is helping you pin down Anton and Herbert. You will arrest them for attempted murder, but you are waiting to find out what they are smuggling out of Italy. The police in Marghera are monitoring three ships due to sail to Spain, Portugal, and South America in the next seven days. You still have not figured out how they knew so much of the Mustaki-Schwartz estate and whether Anton knew already that Elena Finci was coming to Venice or whether he found out because they were watching the countess. Bruno told you they knew a lot about the inheritance."

Umberto De Antoni had started using Rachele's method to figure things out. He took out his notepad with all the circles, opened it, and showed it to her.

"I have figured out a lot of things. Colonel McLaren told us that his office employed Herbert as a cleaner; he might have found the letter that Guido Schwartz sent his son. It is likely that his father's letter arrived not more than a day or two after Joshua left Vienna, otherwise the mailroom would have known that he had gone. They must have an inside source to know so much about the Pesaro De Bonfili household. I have not figured out how the three of them came together, not that it is relevant to what they are doing now. I am just curious."

Rachele returned the notepad, took her own out, and started looking for the page where she had written some notes. She smiled when she found it.

"Bruno and Herbert knew each other, or at least Bruno said that it was Herbert who pointed out that he looked like an officer in one of the US occupation forces offices he cleaned. Bruno's wife had already told him he reminded her of some photos of her father when he was young, long before she was born. So, when Bruno heard the officer's name, he wondered whether the officer was related to his late father-in-law. I do not know what the connection between Bruno and Herbert is. Maybe Colonel McLaren can give us the information they have on Herbert. They must have vetted him before hiring him. Has Bruno mentioned anything?"

"Bruno does not talk much about his teammates, only about their plans."

"Can you contact Colonel McLaren, or do we ask Joshua?"

"My English is not good enough. Joshua has an official capacity in the investigation. He is the liaison officer between the Venetian police and the US Army office in Vienna. He talks to Colonel McLaren."

"So, we ask Joshua. We need to figure out how they knew so much about the comings and goings of Aunt Deborah's household. How did they know that the young woman we then knew as Leah Schwartz would arrive in Venice? How did they know that Joshua Schwartz had arrived? How did they know when they were going out and where they were going? They now perceive Joshua as a threat; the last attempt at his life could not be mistaken as an accident."

Umberto De Antoni stopped writing notes and closed the other notepad he had with him. He reached for his briefcase and took out a diary.

"I think you have just formulated an action plan (1) Joshua contacts Colonel McLaren, (2) I ask Bruno for information about his teammates next time we speak, which is in an hour from now, and (3) you have a chat with the countess trying to find out more about her household staff. They must have an insider in that household; we just need to figure out who that person is. We meet and compare notes Thursday morning unless we must act sooner because of their smuggling activities, but I hope we do not because we need to know who tells them what the Pesaro De Bonfili household is doing."

He wrote the action points as he was saying them; he then closed the diary, put it back in his briefcase, closed it, and was ready to leave. Rachele looked at her watch; he had said he needed forty-five minutes and, so far, he had been in the office for forty. She closed her notepad and stood up. Before they left the office, she added.

"I would rule out her housekeeper, but I do not know who else she employs. I shall discuss her household with her next time we meet for coffee."

On their way to the door, Gabriele appeared. He and Rachele invited Umberto and his wife to lunch in November, provided they brought the baby with them. After they closed the door, Rachele looked at her watch and smiled. The Vice-Commissario had been in their office for forty-five minutes!

Countess Pesaro De Bonfili was thrilled; the court accepted the petition to adopt Elena Finci. Nothing would change since she was her legal guardian, but the future looked different. However slow Italian bureaucracy might have been, they still had over four years before Elena became a legal adult. An adoption would then become problematic, not impossible, but more complicated from a bureaucratic point of view. A very happy Deborah Camerini joined Rachele in their usual place for coffee. It was too cold to sit outside in the courtyard; they sat at a corner table in the back. Rachele sat next to the back door with her back against the wall and a full view of the entrance; her honorary aunt remarked she had not lost the habits she had acquired during her time in the resistance. That day, the countess seemed to have no intention of discussing the Mustaki-Schwartz inheritance or any event associated with it. Still, Rachele had to discuss it with her. The police had declared Joshua's last accident an attempted murder. Something that had to be investigated.

"Vice-Commissario De Antoni and I were wondering how Anton and Herbert could know so much about the movements in your household. I told him I was confident that your housekeeper would not do anything to harm you or your guests. Who else are you employing?"

Rachele knew that her honorary aunt would appreciate her trust in the housekeeper, who kept her safe during the German occupation and protected her assets, as Anita had done for them. Deborah Camerini had thought about it herself.

"As you know, I trusted Tonia with my life, but I wondered whether she might have given relevant information to the wrong person. However, it was quite clear their knowledge of what Joshua, Elena, and I were doing and where we were going could not have come from random information gathered from overhearing Tonia chatting to somebody on the street."

The countess took a sip of her coffee; she continued with a grin.

"I would also exclude my bookkeeper because he is my honorary nephew and your husband. I think we could both trust Gabriele, can't we?"

Rachele smiled, but the remark showed that the countess was mildly annoyed, not mad, just slightly irritated. Deborah Camerini drank a sip of water and smiled back at her honorary niece before continuing.

"Other people come and go, but at random moments, so they would not be a regular source of information."

It was quite clear that she was going through a list.

"My live-in maid is a young woman from Monselice; the Germans shot her father as part of a retaliation for a grenade thrown at a truck full of German soldiers. A cousin of Tonia introduced her family to us; I will ask Tonia if she knows whether she has a suitor. She could unintentionally provide information. Rosa comes in the morning to help with the cleaning and stays till lunchtime. She is a refugee from Zara who only works three hours a day when her children are in school. Either Tonia or Gabriele would know how to reach her. Gabriele prepares the envelope with cash twice a month, and I am sure Tonia has her address. You can ask either of them. I will tell Tonia to call you and give you any information you ask."

Rachele noticed the cleaner had a name, but the countess described her live-in maid, but did not say her name.

"What is the name of the girl from Monselice?"

The countess smiled, embarrassed.

"She is called Cristina, and I call her Tina. Unfortunately, she shares her first name with the wife of the German Colonel, who lived in my home for a year and a half. An arrogant lady of no upbringing who treated the woman she knew as Tonia's mother (that would have been me) as if she did not exist or as if she were an unnecessary burden. I now hate that name."

Rachele smiled at the thought of anybody treating Countess Deborah Pesaro De Bonfili as if she did not exist. Rachele added 'talk to Tonia' to her notes. She would discuss it with Umberto De Antoni first, but she thought she had more chances to have a relaxed conversation with her honorary aunt's housekeeper than a policeman.

Vice-Commissario Umberto De Antoni was on his way to Rachele's office. It was a warm October evening; the sunset made the buildings facing the Grand Canal glow. A middle-aged American couple was sitting outside next to him on the back of the vaporetto; the man was taking photographs. Umberto felt privileged to almost live in this place of beauty. He came every day from Mestre[4] to work here. The bus ride to Piazzale Roma was most definitely not the highlight of his day, but being in a vaporetto looking at the city had not become a habit yet. The young man from a small town near Udine was still in awe of *'La Serenissima'*[5], the most serene city. He got off the vaporetto in a great mood, looking forward to talking to Rachele. He walked up the stairs to the office two steps at a time. Rachele opened the door and steered him to the kitchen for coffee. Once they moved to her office, Rachele had news for him.

"I think we are close to unravelling all of this and figuring out who is involved in the attempted murder of Joshua Schwartz. The Pesaro De Bonfili household employs the housekeeper and two other women. A live-in maid, Cristina Natali from Monselice, called Tina, and another maid that comes in the morning, Rosa Draghi, a refugee from Zara. Gabriele knows how to reach her because he prepares an envelope with cash every month. Draghi sounds an awful lot like Draeger or Dragovich, don't you think?"

Vice Commissario Umberto De Antoni stopped taking notes.

"It looks too easy. Do you know how Tina came to be employed by the countess? Why does Gabriele prepare an envelope for Rosa Draghi? Aren't maids paid in cash on the day?"

Everybody else had gone home, so the door to Rachele's office was open; Gabriele appeared at the door as if they had summoned him.

Chapter Nineteen

November 1948

I t was a foggy day, the sort of fog that makes everything look out of focus. Federico Teglio was walking towards his office in the commercial port when he noticed a ship flying an Argentinian Flag. He did not remember her being there the previous day. It was eight-thirty in the morning; Zvi's aunt was likely to be at work, according to what his friend had told him. He thought his willingness to help might be useful one day, either with the police or the Cantoni-Mendes-Modiano law firm. Once he was in his office, he dialled the number of the law firm. As expected, Gabriele picked it up. He introduced himself and asked him to pass a message to Rachele. Gabriele wrote it down, asked for his phone number, and told him that either Rachele or Vice-Commissario Umberto De Antoni would call him back if they needed to ask him anything.

After putting down the phone, Gabriele went to the kitchen where his wife and their friend were having coffee. He related the message and went back to his bookkeeping. It was the beginning of the month, a time to look at overdue invoices and make calls. Rachele and Umberto moved to her office and closed the door, so the greetings of people coming to work would not interrupt them. The ship from South America was a new development; however, Rachele felt that there was another equally important question that needed an answer.

"I am sure you realise that without a link between Anton or Herbert and the Pesaro De Bonfili household, you do not have enough evidence to charge them with the attempted murder of Joshua Schwartz. You told me you still have not figured out what they are smuggling out of Italy. Gabriele has the telephone number of Zvi's friend; we may ask him to find out when the ship is due to sail and what her next port is."

The Vice-Commissario pointed to the circle marked "Tina and Rosa".

"We looked at Rosa Draghi; we have found no obvious connection with Anton Draeger/Ante Dragovich. Your nephew told me that when Mussolini suggested that people with a foreign sounding last names should change it into something that sounded more Italian, many people changed their Slav or German-sounding last names. We have asked the Yugoslavian authorities in Zara to help trace birth certificates to check whether Draghi is the Italian-sounding equivalent of a Croatian name, but are not holding our breath. We have been watching the comings and goings of the two young women for a week; Tina meets the same young man when she goes out to run errands in the afternoon. We have asked Tomia, the housekeeper, and she thinks Tina organises her life to run errands before dinner."

Rachele wrote 'Tina's young man' in one of her circles. They continued discussing other possibilities; in the end, Umberto De Antoni decided to find out when the Argentinian ship was supposed to sail and what her destination was. They bumped into Franco Cantoni as they left Rachele's office. Umberto had an idea; he would call Alex and Franco later that morning, after he checked something.

~

Alex and Franco had agreed to be with the policeman who was watching the back door to the Pesaro De Bonfili residence. Franco was the only one who had seen Herbert several times. They were sitting at a café in Strada Nova, near the junction with Calle Fontana, where the countess lived; the plainclothes policeman had been talking to Franco and Alex as if he had been a long-lost friend but never averted his eyes from the Calle. They had already paid the bill to be free to leave with no notice. Tina came out of the alleyway carrying an empty shopping bag. They stood up, ready to follow her at a distance. The fog had cleared up during the day; there were few people around; the policeman was sure they would not lose her. She turned a corner into a junction wide enough to have a newsagent in the middle; she stopped by the newsagent and warmly greeted a young man. He was wearing a large hat that partially hid his face, and he had to push it back to kiss Tina. Alex recognised the man. They had the link, but not the one they expected.

Vice Commissario Umberto de Antoni was having coffee with Rachele, Alex, and Franco. He had stopped by to tell them they had made arrests. Thanks to Federico Teglio, they stopped Anton Draeger/Ante Dragovich/Antonio Draghi from boarding a ship that was scheduled to sail to Argentina three days later. Countess Pesaro De Bonfili was due to join them with Elena Finci and Joshua Schwartz. Rachele now had all her circles tidied up in order; she was ready to explain everything.

They were all assembled in the meeting room overlooking the Grand Canal, almost twelve months to the day after Deborah Camerini, Countess Pesaro De Bonfili, had brought them the wills. They still had to regain possession of many assets the court had agreed to give back to the estate, so that matter was not closed. However, she had to tell them they had no more reason to fear for their lives or be cautious. The Vice-Commissario was there because he wanted to hear just in case he had missed some detail that might come in handy later. Rachele was sitting at the head of the table; her partners were as curious as her guests. Gabriele was not sure he had the whole story; Franco had promised to tell everything to the receptionist, who could not leave her desk or the phone. Once they had coffee and eaten the refreshments, Rachele was ready to explain.

"At the moment, I feel like Hercule Poirot in an Agatha Christie book, but…."

Alex Modiano's quick wit got the best of him; he just could not resist

"Why not Miss Marple?"

"Do you see me as a quaint old lady tending roses in the front garden in an English country village?"

Deborah Camerini came to her defence.

"I think you are as far from Miss Marple as possible; I would see you more like a glamorous and slim equivalent of Nero Wolfe."

Rachele smiled, tried to look at everybody as if they were hostile witnesses, and continued.

"Well, literary comparisons aside, I am afraid that the estate and the inheritance were a ploy to get to Joshua. In Vienna, he worked in the allied task force, looking for Nazis. They expanded their search to Ustasha, following a request of the Russians, who were asked by the Yugoslavian Tito government. That put Ante Dragovich on their radar, except they had no recent photograph of him, and they did not know that he was now calling himself Anton Draeger pretending to be an Austrian refugee. Ante had already secured his wife and younger children in South America. Running an operation smuggling Ustasha and their families to South America kept him in Europe. He had always hidden from the US Army because his son-in-law Herbert Platzich had found a job as a maintenance man in the US Army building where Colonel McLaren and Joshua Schwartz had their offices."

Joshua Interrupted her

"The connection between Herbert and his father-in-law should have come out when the US Army checked him."

Rachele smiled and continued

"They knew him as Herbert Platz from Graz, and there was no marriage certificate under that name. Somehow, nobody checked that there was also no birth certificate. Herbert's first cousin, Bruno Heber, looked a lot like Joshua. Two days before Joshua announced he was returning to the United States, he saw Herbert and Anton/Ante sitting in a café together. There was no actual conversation, just a polite greeting."

Joshua couldn't help himself.

"Why did they make me a threat?"

This time Rachele did not smile, she just looked at him in a way that sent a clear message.

"The following morning, Herbert made the mistake of telling you he was sitting with his father-in-law. It turned out that Colonel McLaren had received information that Ante Dragovich was also using the name Anton Draeger. You did not know you had become the only person who had seen Ante/Anton. Herbert could not remember whether he had introduced his father-in-law or mentioned his name, but you were supposed to travel to the United States the following day. So, he thought little of it until he found the letter from your father asking you to go to Venice on your empty desk."

Joshua had to ask, but he also had to show he had got the previous message.

"Sorry, Rachele, is that why they brought Bruno to Venice to impersonate me?"

By now Rachele had started accepting interruption with some grace.

"Exactly. Ante remembered that Herbert's cousin looked like you, so he thought of sending Bruno to Venice, pretending to be Joshua. They knew that sooner or later Joshua would appear in Venice, and they had decided to use Bruno Heber as a byte."

The countess was drinking water. She put down the glass.

"But Elena's accidents started before Joshua arrived in Venice."

Once again, Rachele smiled, hoping to send the silent message to be patient.

"They could not imagine that by a series of unexpected and fortuitous circumstances, a survivor of Nazi persecution of Greek Jews would appear in Venice, one of the few who could place Ante/Anton in the SS. What happened on the ship that was taking Jews from the island of Rhodes to the transit camp near Athens must have been very vivid in Ante/Anton's mind because he recognised Elena when she arrived with Rabbi Lazar and his wife. He thought it was a lucky coincidence that he was at the station with Herbert, waiting for people coming from Trieste. He did not know that Elena had lost her memory. Herbert followed Elena to the Pesaro de Bonfili residence. Now he knew where she was staying; he had to find a way to get inside information without exposing himself."

"So, they now had two people that were a threat, both of them connected to me. How did you find out about their machinations?"

"Bruno Heber has been co-operating very effectively with the police and is now being assisted by us. Anyway, Herbert had a great idea to ask for help from one of the guest house staff where they were staying. Herbert had already established that the Pesaro De Bonfili household employed a young woman as a live-in maid, so he thought of the receptionist of the hotel where Bruno was staying. So, he asked the young man to see if he could court her and get information about the coming and going of the Pesaro De Bonfili household. At the time, they did not know that Joshua Schwartz was also connected to the Pesaro De Bonfili family. They had an extra person to consider. They thought they hit the conspirators' jackpot when Joshua arrived because he stayed at aunt Deborah's. By the way, Bruno Heber does not know that, but they had decided to get rid of him when we figured out that he was not Joshua Schwartz. The first thing they did not know was that we were working with Vice-Commissario De Antoni, and we enlisted Bruno to spy for us with some protection."

Alex looked at Joshua Schwartz, who was listening very carefully; for once, the countess had no intention of being centre stage. Vice-Commissario Umberto De Antoni was ready to take notes, just in case Rachele revealed a detail he did not know. Everybody was concentrating on what Rachele was saying. Franco, however, had a question.

"What else did they not know?"

Rachele had known Franco all his life. She had no problem telling him to be patient. It was a complicated story. She sipped some water, then she resumed.

"They knew Elena had lost her memory, but they could not trust her. What would happen when she recovered her memory? Herbert was not very good at getting rid of Elena, so Ante enlisted somebody else who came from South America; the blond man Zvi and Federico Teglio saw leave a ship between Bruno and Herbert. They thought they had got rid of Joshua when he was thrown off a bridge after being hit from behind. Somehow even the blond man was sloppy and did not know that Joshua had not hit the water but ended up on the Fondamenta, breaking a few bones but still alive."

Rachele noticed Umberto De Antoni was taking notes. They knew something the police did not, whatever that something was.

"We knew Herbert was involved with scaring Elena because Franco saw him; we thought they were behind the attempts to get rid of Joshua, but we did not know their connection with the Pesaro De Bonfili household. They were too familiar with the comings and goings of Elena, Joshua, and Countess Deborah. They kept their deal with the receptionist from Bruno Heber and never talked about it when he was around. The police suspected there was a connection between the Pesaro De Bonfili household and them, but did not know what it was. We assumed they had some inside information, but when Alex recognised the man Tina was seeing regularly as the receptionist of the hotel where Bruno was staying, the police had watertight evidence of the connection between them and the household."

Elena felt she had to say something to support Tina.

"Tina has been crying over her misplaced love for the past few days."

Rachele was annoyed but had a soft spot for Elena. She drank some water, hoping to look as if she had planned the interruption.

"The receptionist did not want to be involved in an attempted murder, so he told the police everything he knew. Tina was very cooperative and aunt Deborah has assured me she will not lose her job. Bruno will serve very little time, considering he has no other offences. Joshua and his father agreed to give twenty per cent of the Mustaki-Schwartz inheritance to his wife, the illegitimate daughter of Joshua's grandfather and, therefore, Joshua's aunt."

Rachele had finished. Vice-Commissario De Antoni closed his notebook. Roberto Mendes, Joshua and the countess were ready to ask questions, but the receptionist interrupted the meeting and asked for Gabriele; Gabriele left for a few minutes and came back with a sombre face. He apologised to the others and asked Rachele and Alex to join him outside for a moment.

"That was Anita on the phone. Baron Davide Modiano passed away in his sleep. Esther rang home and spoke with Anita, who rang us. Alex, your father, is the new Baron Modiano. We must go home and prepare to leave for Trieste as soon as possible."

Chapter Twenty

March - April 1949

Leo and Mario insisted they wanted to go to the station to meet Elena, who was on the night train from Vienna. Gabriele and Rachele had agreed to sign letters excusing them from the first half of their school day. The arrangement was that they would go to school earlier than expected if the train was late. Elena was travelling back to Venice with Joshua Schwartz and the countess after being a witness at the trial of Ante Dragovich/Anton Draeger/Antonio Draghi. The war criminal that she could identify as the SS who shot her siblings in cold blood and other atrocities during the transport of Rhodes Jews to the transit camp in Greece. She also testified that he shot people who were too slow getting on the freight wagons that took them to Auschwitz/Birkenau.

The train was on time. Leo and Mario saw Joshua helping the porter with the luggage, the countess, and Elena emerging from the train. They ran towards them and hugged Elena. The countess smiled at the welcoming committee, asking for a hug. Joshua was busy dealing with the porter and smiled at them. Elena was walking out of the station between Leo and Mario, who had grown very protective of her. The countess was watching them, smiling. She remarked to Joshua that they were the next generation to follow a tradition. Her daughter Sarah and Myriam Mendes were the same age; they had been close friends since childhood. She and Fiamma had been friends since school. Leo, Elena, and Mario were following in their footsteps.

~

Two days later, the Countess, Rachele, and Joshua Schwartz were at the law firm to discuss the progress in retrieving the assets. Courts might have judged in their favour, but the bureaucracy of re-acquiring ownership of the properties was slow. They were waiting for Alvise, Franco, and Alex to join them after they had updated the list of assets. Rachele wanted to know about Elena in Vienna; the countess was full of maternal pride.

"You should have seen her. She kept saying she knew what she saw, and nobody could confuse her; it was her turn to fight. In court, she was very calm and told the story without tears or signs of anxiety. The trial was in English; Joshua was about to be sworn in as an interpreter, but the defence objected. Elena said she had learned English in the Displacement People camp after the war; she did not need an interpreter. If she did not understand one question, she would just ask for it to be explained to her."

"Was she nervous?"

"She was very calm during the two days leading to her taking the stand as a witness. When they asked her if she saw the man who shot her brother in the courthouse, she pointed her finger at Ante and said that he had blond hair, but people can die their hair. It was most definitely him. She could not forget his face or his voice saying *Jetzt Schwimm*[1] after he threw her dead brother's body overboard."

"What happened afterwards?"

"She sat on the witness stand in silence; she looked at me and smiled. When the judge excused her, she ran to me, hugged me, and was fighting tears. The judge thanked her and praised her ability to stay calm. It was only after dinner when I wished her good night that she started crying."

Joshua added that the following morning at breakfast, she told him she felt lighter; she felt Leah had saved her for something.

Elena Finci had asked to talk to Aunt Rachele in her office. She had a legal question to ask, and she wanted the countess and her two children, Giorgio, and Sarah, to be there when she asked Rachele, who had no idea why Elena wanted everybody around her. When she arrived with the Countess, Rachele noticed Elena was as immaculately turned out as her adoptive mother. They did not have to wait long until Giorgio and Sarah appeared. Nobody had seen Elena so in control since they met her about a year earlier. Her demeanour and her voice spelt confidence. Everybody was sitting down in the meeting room overlooking the Grand Canal. Elena sat between Giorgio and Sarah; she adjusted her posture as if she knew she had just gone on stage.

"Aunt Rachele, I have a question for you regarding my adoption, but first, I need Giorgio and Sarah's consent. When Aunt Deborah, sorry my mother…I am sorry; it is a habit that I will lose one day. When my mother told me she wanted to adopt me, I asked her to keep my last name. I felt it was a way to honour my family. Now I think I have honoured my Greek family in Vienna. So, Giorgio, Sarah, do you mind if I ask if it is too complicated to change my last name to Pesaro De Bonfili after the court has approved the adoption?"

Nobody expected that. The countess took a handkerchief from her handbag and started dabbing her eyes, trying not to smudge her makeup with the tears she felt coming. Sarah did not have her mother's concern; she was touched. Giorgio smiled and hugged her, and Sarah hugged her as well. Giorgio felt he had to say something; he straightened himself up, looked at his mother, smiled, and turned to Elena with a serious voice and a smiling face.

"My little sister, you are part of our family, whatever name you want to use. Still, I am so happy you want to use ours."

Sarah hugged her again. Elena was pleased; she turned to Rachele and asked how complicated it was to amend their petition for adoption. Rachele pointed out that her adoptive mother had to sign it; at the court hearing, she would have to state that she agreed to take the Pesaro De Bonfili family name. A note from her brother and sister saying they would not object would help.

Twice a week, after they had done their homework and before dinner, Elena would meet Leo, Mario, and their friends at an ice cream place at the Zattere. That day, Elena had asked if she could do her homework with Leo and Mario and then go to the ice cream place together. On their way to Zattere, they talked about their homework and how she was doing catching up with her tutors. They were waiting for her in their class the following October. Once they reached Campo dei Frari, Elena stopped them.

"I have asked Aunt Rachele to ask the court to change my last name to Pesaro De Bonfili when they finalise the adoption."

Leo reacted with a smile and a teasing tone in his voice

"Do we have to call you the new countess?"

Elena lightly punched Leo on his left arm.

Mario did not want to be late to meet their friends. He started walking again but felt he had to react, just to tease Leo,

"But the new countess will be Samuel's wife and Samuel Pesaro De Bonfili is not four yet."

Elena looked at him with a huge grin

"Precisely!"

The three of them continued walking to the Zattere.

When they were back home, Leo remarked to Anita that Elena did not stay between him and Mario all the time, and when they were at the ice cream place, she sat on the opposite bench, next to two other girls.

Joshua and the countess were at the airport waiting to meet Guido Schwartz. Joshua's father had decided to meet the sister he had never met before. His wife had decided not to come. Their daughter was attending Brown University, but their youngest son was still in school. He noticed his son waving from inside the terminal, took his hat off, and started waving it in the air to be more visible. It was his first time in Venice since they left for the United States in 1936. He had kept in touch with his honorary aunt, the wife of his father's closest friend. Almost thirteen years later, he still knew his place. He hugged his son and took a step back to look at the countess.

"Aunt Deborah, you look like I remember you before we left for the United States."

Deborah Camerini replied in a coy voice.

"You are very smooth, Guido. Do you mind if I call you Guido? I have no idea whether you have anglicised your name like your son. I have hired a porter for your luggage."

She started walking with the porter towards the water taxis, leaving space for father and son to catch up. When they arrived at the Pesaro De Bonfili residence, Guido walked in with a huge smile.

"I remember this place very well. Some of my earliest memories of Venice are tied to this place."

The countess told Tonia to leave the luggage in the hall, then turned to Guido.

"This place turned you into a Venetian. You met your wife here, although I cannot claim I planned the match."

Joshua looked at his father, and they both smiled. When Elena arrived from one of her lessons, Guido greeted his new 'honorary cousin.' Elena smiled, delighted for yet another recognition that she was part of the family.

It was not spring yet, but the weather signalled winter was over. Gabriele, Rachele, Alvise, and Roberto were discussing the Schwartz estate in the meeting room facing the Grand Canal. The sun's reflection from the water was drawing shapes on the ceiling. Shapes were changing every time a boat passed through their bit of the Grand Canal. Gabriele was reviewing the list of assets he had in front of him. He was ticking the items they had already completely recovered. The partners had divided the work to regain possession of the assets amongst themselves. Whenever he mentioned something they had not yet fully recovered, the partner taking care of it would update the others on how much the law firm had worked on it and how much work was still necessary. Gabriele compared that with the value of the assets. They were getting ready for a meeting with Guido Schwartz later that morning.

Alvise stood up, collected the used cups and saucers and took them to the kitchen to come back with fresh coffee; Roberto took the opportunity of the break to stand and walked to the window and noticed the countess and Elena getting off the vaporetto.

"I did not know we were expecting aunt Deborah and Elena, now."

The unexpected arrival of the countess triggered the usual panic. Gabriele and Roberto tidied the table; Rachele rushed to the bathroom to check her appearance. She saw Alvise coming out of the kitchen and mentioned aunt Deborah shouting it to make sure everybody else in the office heard it and would act accordingly; they thought they had another hour. Franco walked out of the room he and Alex shared.

"I asked Elena to come earlier; I need her help to get paperwork from Rhodes; informally, I communicate in Italian, but now that I need official paperwork, they are switching to Greek for their records. I need Elena, and the countess decided to come as well."

Alvise told his son he should have mentioned it. They relaxed a bit; Franco smiled when he saw the receptionist checking that her desk and appearance were fit to be inspected by Deborah Camerini.

Franco came out of his room before the receptionist had finished helping the countess and Elena with their coats. By that time, Gabriele, Roberto, and Rachele had come out of their room to greet their honorary aunt and their honorary cousin. They were relieved to hear that the countess was there because she and Elena had an appointment with Mrs Toffolo later that morning. Gabriele felt he needed to explain they were using the meeting room overlooking the Grand Canal to prepare for the meeting with Guido Schwartz, so Franco would take them to the other meeting room.

An hour later, Guido and Joshua Schwartz arrived. By now, Joshua had become a friend of Alex and Franco and part of the extended Mendes clan, so the social side took some time. The meeting was long; every asset they had not completely recovered yet had to be assessed against its value, the bureaucratic process, and the cost. Alvise reminded them they were liable to pay taxes on every asset now that the court had ruled in favour of restitution. Raffaele Mustaki's estate was subject to double duty, the one his wife Sylvia would have paid and the one that Sylvia's heir had to pay. Guido listened to everything while Joshua was taking notes. It took two hours to review the list; Guido thanked everybody and turned to Gabriele.

"I know you keep Aunt Deborah's books; please ensure the estate reimburses her for all her expenses, including the costs of protecting Joshua and Elena. Also, if it is not a conflict of interest, I would like to retain you as the bookkeeper for my business interests in Italy. Joshua has decided to stay in Venice for a while, and he will manage the estate."

He then turned to the partners with different instructions.

"I want to create a holding company for all our interests in Italy, including the factory near Treviso and the real estate. That should also include what I inherited from my father and did not sell when we moved to the States but transferred to a Swiss company. May I have a plan for that a few days before I leave at the end of the month? I like to discuss it with you, and I do not dare leave aunt Deborah out of the conversation. Also, tomorrow Joshua and I will travel to Trieste. Sylvia and I discovered we had a sister when my father's will was read in Trieste in 1936. It took us a while to process it; then, I moved to the United States. Sylvia wanted to meet her, but racial laws made travelling complicated for Jews. Then the war happened. We have waited too long; by 'we', I mean Sylvia and I. Now it's time. Angela will choose whether to take the twenty per cent we have decided to set aside for her in cash, shares in the holding company, or a combination of both. "

Roberto said that they would have a plan by the following week, and his brother was already keeping books for two other clients of the firm. He was meticulous in justifying any payment to the firm and always double-checked his clients' bills before preparing the invoice.

Rachele and the countess had enjoyed meetings for coffee once a week. So, they continued even if there were no more mysteries surrounding the Mustaki-Schwartz estate, and Elena's adoption process was moving along with no problems. So, they met while Elena had her lesson with one of her tutors nearby. The only difference was that she would join them at the end of her lesson, with no bodyguard, no need to hide or be weary. It was ten days before Passover, and both the countess and Rachele were enjoying baked goods in the café's courtyard. The day was perfect for sitting outside, even though they kept their coats on. Rachele was praising the savoury tart she was eating. The countess remarked that since it came from Anna's patisserie; she was not expecting anything else. She then moved to her news.

"Joshua is settling in Venice. He is keeping a car in the big car park in Piazzale Roma and is looking for his own place. He has a long list of requirements, so I do not expect him to move out soon. I am thrilled that Elena is coming to you for the second night of Passover, and Fiamma invited Joshua and me. Elena will turn seventeen this year. She needs the company of her peers, not her ageing mother!"

Rachele smiled inwardly at the 'ageing mother' comment. Deborah Camerini rarely admitted that she was growing old, like all the other mortals. Still, she had to tease her honorary aunt.

"Do you have any young woman to invite for a Friday night dinner before Joshua moves out?"

The countess smiled, picked up her mirror, and checked her make-up. Rachele saw through those tactics. Deborah Camerini was buying time. She then put the mirror back in her handbag and looked at Rachele with a mischievous grin.

"My dear, I did not plan my most successful match. Anyway, how old is Dina's sister? Maybe it is time I invite her to dinner."

Afterthoughts

This is not the last book I plan to write featuring the Modiano/Mendes clan or the Pesaro De Bonfili family. As I was writing it, the idea of two series took shape in my mind. So, in the future you will have:

1. Rachele Modiano Mendes, the early years. A collection of novellas that will take Gabriele, Rachele, and, in due course, their children up to 1940. The first book in the series "Reflection in the Water" was published in September 2023.
2. Rachele Modiano Mendes investigates. A collection of novels that will take place between 1947 and 1985, when my grandmother, the inspiration for Rachele Modiano Mendes, took 'early retirement' from the law at 88. This is the first book.

Both series will be cosy crime stories. "The Dressmaker's Parcels" almost stands as the bridge between the two. If you are so inclined, you can share your views and comments on this and other stories by leaving a comment on the "Books" page of my blog: https://authorsilvano.substack.com/p/books.

I do not have a website yet; it is one of my project for tomorrow. I shall announce when "tomorrow" morphs into "today" in my blog.

Acknowledgments

There may be only one author, but it takes a village to publish a book. I need to acknowledge my beta-readers, Andrea Rosen, Eyal Ducamp, Daniella Pinkstein, Nahum Schnitzer and Fabrizio Soggetto. There are not enough words to express my appreciation of their feedback, and their encouragement..

Fabrizio Soggetto was more than a beta reader. His notes were so detailed that it was more like having a developmental editor. I am very lucky he agreed to read the manuscript.

It took me three years to publish my first book. I wrote other stories during that time. Now I look like an extremely prolific writer. In reality, 2023 production has been three years in the making. I would not have made it if London Writers' Salon had not come into my life. It has become an important part of the village that took me here.

The London Writers' Salon makes writing less solitary. Up to four times a day, you are one of several squares in a Zoom screen. It's magic. Try it if you do not believe it. It is also a source of friends who provide encouragement. We bounce ideas off each other, talking about what we write once a week. The Gold coaches Katryn, Niamh, Eimar, and Anna support you and help you get unstuck or recover your motivation on bad days. Fellow gold members are a group of cheerleaders that support you and cheer you. Whether the journey is long or short, I would not have been able to do it without them.

Recently I started running a group within that London Writers' Salon that meets once a month discussing self-publishing, Print On Demand, and promoting books. Talking to members of this group gave me many ideas, and I have learnt so much. I am deeply grateful to each and every one of them.

Last but by no means least, there are a few backstories in this book. I hope I have done justice to the feelings of people who survived World War II, whatever happened to them during that time. My parents belonged to the generation just starting in life in the second half of the forties. I hope I expressed the respect I have for that generation, Jews and non-Jews, civilians, or military, who had to rebuild (or build) their lives after five (or six) years of a conflict that was devastating for everybody, whether they were combatants or civilians.

Notes

Chapter 3

1. Literally to make the ascent, a way to indicate that they moved to Israel.
2. The territories that became a part of Italy at the end of the first World War had been part of the Austrian Empire for centuries. Italians, Slovenians, Croatians, Germans, and other nations part of the Austrian Empire had freely mixed.

   After World War II, Italy had to give Yugoslavia a strip of territory, sometimes only a few kilometres wide, in the northern part of the border. However, the Istrian Peninsula became a part of Yugoslavia, except for a narrow slither of land around Trieste that became a separate political entity run by the Allied forces. Like Austria and Germany, the British and the Americans ran Zone A of the Free Territory of Trieste together; Yugoslavia administered Zone B.

   During the timeframe of the story (between 1947 and 1949), the Free Territory of Trieste was a separate political entity from Italy. A passport was required to travel between Trieste and Italy. In 1954, the allied transferred the administration of Zone A to Italy. The Treaty of Osimo defined the border between Italy and Yugoslavia only in 1975, and the two countries ratified the Treaty in 1977.

Chapter 4

1. The nickname comes from the days of the Republic of Venice, also known as the most serene republic of Venice.
2. Ritual circumcision of a baby boy; it usually take place when the baby is eight days old, unless there are health complications.

Chapter 6

1. See note 3 on page 21

Chapter 7

1. In 1948, high school leavers in Italy had the so-called "Esami di Maturita' "(Maturity exams), a nightmare for all who remember them. Teenagers would spend Mid May and the whole of June studying the whole curriculum of 12 subjects with written and oral tests in all subjects, keeping them busy for the first three weeks in July.

Chapter 9

1. *The Betrothed* by Alessandro Manzoni is a novel written in the XIX century that takes place in Milan in the seventeenth century. The Unnamed is a nobleman so feared by everybody that his name could only be pronounced as a whisper in somebody's ears. The book has been a compulsory reading in Italian high schools for a long time. It is considered one of Italian literature's most important works of fiction.

Chapter 11

1. 1945 and 1946 saw most ethnic Italians leave the territories that had become part of Yugoslavia. The beginning of the Cold War between Russia and the Allies shaped the events. Yugoslavia was aligned with Russia. Many Italians chose to leave or were 'assertively invited to leave.' In those days, many people seized any opportunity to settle scores. Many ethnic Italians or Italian sympathisers in that area were buried in caves, the so-called 'Foibe'. Some of them were buried alive.

Chapter 12

1. In the forties, fifties and sixties, Italian schoolchildren were given "homework" to complete during their summer holidays. In those days, the Italian summer school holidays lasted from mid-June to October 1st.

Chapter 14

1. The Ustasha was a Croatian nationalist movement that nominally ruled the independent republic of Croatia after the German and the Italian partitioned the Kingdom of Yugoslavia during World War II.

   The Ustasha also conscripted an army to join the Axis powers (Germany, Italy, and Japan) and to fight the resistance movements that operating in the Yugoslav territory. They remained nominally in control until May 1945, when the German army collapsed, and its followers fled, fearing retaliation from the communist partisans led by Tito.

Chapter 15

1. In Italy, married women do not formally change their last name; in any official paper where men have "married," women had their husband's last name. Rachele Modano was married to Gabriele Mendes, but, professionally, she was still "Avvocato Rachele Modiano" "Avvocato" (the Italian word for "lawyer") is used as her title.

2. In the aftermath of World War II, the Italian eastern border was moved west, and former Italian territories became part of Yugoslavia. The Istria peninsula, mainly in modern-day Croatia, used to be part of Italy. Most of the ethnic Italians or Italian speakers left the area in 1946, but there was still a sizeable minority left, especially in some parts of Istria. Fiume (or Rijeka in Croatian), the city on the eastern corner of the "Istria triangle", had, and still has, an Italian minority. In 1948, the area around Trieste was an independent territory under the joint administration of the US and UK.

Chapter 18

1. Fascist Italy's antisemitic laws were different from Germany's. There was no final solution and the laws only impacted members of a Jewish community If Jews got themselves baptized they were not part of a Jewish community and therefore not affected by racial laws. It all changed in September 1943 when Germany extended the final solution to Italian and Hungarian Jews. The Holocaust arrived in Italy in September 1943, for Northern Italy it lasted 18 months. 85% of Italian Jews survived.
2. Shanah Tovah, a good year. It is one of the greetings Jews exchange around the Jewish New Year. It is a way to wish the other person a good year. One of the other is "I wish you a good and sweet new year."
3. In Venetian dialect, those who live in the old city are called *"Veneziani d'acqua"* (Venetians of the water), those who live in the mainland, Mestre, are called *"Veneziani di terra"* (Venetians of the land).
4. Mestre is the 'suburb' of Venice that used to be the town at the other end of the ferry to the mainland; now, it is at the other end of the bridge connecting Venice to the mainland.
5. The Republic of Venice was called "the Most Serene Republic of Venice" (La Serenissima Repubblica di Venezia")

Chapter 20

1. Now Swim

About the Author

Silvano Stagni

Silvano Stagni is a multilingual citizen of the world, a father of four, a cosmopolitan character with a long and varied life. In his youth, he was blessed to have many storytellers, people from different cultures and walks of life. He heard stories from the Imperial Court in Vienna, stories from the Kenyan bush, stories of seafarers, stories of survivors, and stories of fighters. He started writing articles, white papers and opinion pieces during his previous professional life as an expert in the implementation of financial regulations. Now it is his turn to tell stories.

Silvano's blog: https://authorsilvano.substack.com/